Legion Rising

Legionnaire Series – Book 2

Legionnaire Series – Book 2

Legion Rising

Andreas Christensen

Legion Rising

Legionnaire Series – Book 2

Cover: Camilla Design

christensenwriting.com

Legion Rising

Legionnaire Series – Book 2

Legion Rising

Legionnaire Series – Book 2

Accolades for Ghost Legion:

"Knocked it out of the park." Trapper

"What do you get if you mix Starship Troopers and the French Foreign Legion? You get a book like this." Leif E. Dolan

The war continues.

Ethan Wang was born on the first day of the alien invasion. Now he has become a legionnaire, one of just a handful to survive the battle that devastated the Ghost Legion.

Having licked its wounds and recovered, the Legion is now preparing to chase the invaders out of the Solar System, once and for all.

Ethan and the rest of the legionnaires must fight all the way. They are well trained and ready to take the fight to the enemy. But one thing they all begin to realize is that not all of them will make it through alive.

The alien invasion brought humanity together against a common foe – or so it seems. But there are more than immediately meets the eye, and while Ethan firmly believes the enemy must be overcome, he begins to wonder if he's being used as a pawn in another fight. A fight to control the destiny of the human race.

"For a long time, there was Heinlein, Drake, Weber, and some of Ringo's stuff. Add Andreas Christensen." James R. Kratzer

"Andreas keeps getting better and better with each book he writes!" Traci Maynard

Legion Rising

Part 1

1.

Ethan enjoyed staying at home with his mother. Elsie doted on him, cleaning his clothes, and cooking for him whatever he'd like. Every time he met her eyes, she smiled. Yes, it was obvious she enjoyed having him around as well. After almost a year gone it felt good to be home, although as soon as he set foot outside the apartment it just didn't feel quite like home anymore. He'd met up with some of his old friends, but they seemed so different now, and even the streets of his old neighborhood looked different. The same, but different too.

He didn't know how long he had before the Legion recalled him, so he tried to spend each day as if it was the last day before leaving. One day, as he walked by Captain Groves High School, a familiar voice called his name. He turned and saw Dr. Lange, his old history teacher. Ethan waited as the older man walked up to him.

"So, Ethan, I hear you're a military man now. I'm proud of you, son," Dr. Lange said, and gave him an approving look. A veteran of the Lumin War himself, the teacher had always spoken warmly of things like honor, duty, and the obligation to serve humanity. Although he might have certain ideas that weren't altogether sanctioned by the authorities, like calling the Unification a coup, the old man commanded respect and got away with speaking more freely than most would have.

"Tell me, in which branch do you serve?"

"Sir, I... I was rejected by the Defense Forces. In fact, we all were. Seems someone had other plans for us. I serve in the Ghost Legion now." Ethan was surprised at how difficult he found it to tell his old teacher that he'd been rejected by every service from Toilet Cleaners to the Aerospace Corps, but even more surprising was the pride that filled his chest when he told him he was a legionnaire.

"The Ghost Legion... Can't say I've heard of them. Is it a new outfit?" Dr. Lange asked. Ethan nodded.

"Formed up by veterans after the war, it's sort of a semi-official unit," he replied.

"Hmm." The teacher squinted. "Is it any good?"

Ethan puffed out his chest.

"The best, Sir. The very best."

The teacher didn't reply, he just smiled at him.

"Well, I guess you won't be coming in anytime soon to get your high school diploma in order then." Ethan shook his head.

"No sir. I still have more than four years left of my contract. And who knows, many legionnaires choose to stay on, making a career out of it."

"Well, I wish you all the best, Ethan. By the way, do you know where Ariel and Julian ended up? You guys left the same day, didn't you?"

2

Ethan smiled then, thinking of how they had skipped the last few weeks of high school, and how green they'd all been when they set foot inside the Recruitment Office.

"Well sir, actually, we're all legionnaires now. Me and Ariel, we're heavy infantry, and Julian's a tech specialist. We went through much of our basic training together."

"I see. Well, I'm glad you're all okay." The older man extended his hand and gave Ethan a firm grip, holding his hand for a few seconds before letting go.

"Ethan, just remember what you're fighting for. Never forget that." Ethan smiled long after his old teacher had gone. He remembered when the recruiter, Senior Decurion Ford was his name, had taken the three friends to where they departed for basic training. Curiously, he'd said something similar. Ethan wondered if it was just coincidence, or if it was something to do with fighting that over the years changed you, that made you forget what you fought for, and begin to live for the fight itself. He shook his head. Only time would tell. He didn't feel like he'd ever forget his purpose. Looking around, breathing the crisp air of a city that was seeing signs of true spring returning after years of extremely short growth seasons and cold summers due to the after effects of the destruction of the Lumin War, he marveled at the beauty of small things. Kids playing, people talking and laughing, a ray of light shining through the cloudy overcast. He vowed to himself that he'd remember, no matter what happened out there in the cold vastness of Space.

2.

The text had told him to be at the Boatman, a joint just outside Spoke Corners, in an hour. Ariel hadn't said anything more, except that she and Julian were already well into their third beer, and he'd have to catch up. It was a couple of weeks since he'd seen them, and he was beginning to tire of watching mindless TV in the evening or playing shootem up games in his room. His old friends seemed increasingly distant, living lives that were so different from his that it was beginning to get hard to find mutual topics of conversation. Ethan figured getting together with a few fellow legionnaires was just what he needed.

Walking took him half an hour, and he enjoyed the evening quiet of the streets. He entered through the main door, and found the room filled with a symphonic heavy metal variety he hadn't heard in a while. The bar was just what he'd expected; dimmed lights, loud music and a mixed crowd of military and locals.

He caught Ariel waving at him, shouting something he couldn't hear. He walked over and saw the table was filled with a couple of military types he didn't recognize, a small group of locals in fancy clothes; friends of Ariel and Julian from Highland Parks, most likely. Julian scooted over to give him room, and Ethan sat down.

"Here, take this one," he said, handing Ethan a draft beer. Ethan took a swig and swallowed the chilled brew.

"Ahh, just what I needed. Thanks!"

4

They sat for an hour, trading stories and discussing tactics and weapons and ammo and whether nuclear shelling or conventional smart bombs would have been more effective against the Lumins at Titan. The locals disappeared after a while, probably bored with all the military talk, which suited Ethan just fine. He was increasingly feeling the itch to return to duty. He enjoyed the time off, and to be home for a while, but he found that he didn't quite fit in anymore. Spending time with other legionnaires made the feeling disappear instantly, and he enjoyed their company.

"I met Dr. Lange the other day," Ethan told the others. Then he told them about his meeting with their old teacher, and how strange it felt to meet this person that they'd all seen as a step above them. Everything had changed now that they were combat veterans as well, having survived Titan. Ariel suddenly nodded toward the door, and stood up. Ethan turned and saw a legionnaire by the door, scanning the crowd. As soon as the man saw them, he strode across the room straight toward them. Ethan noticed the black D on his lapel, and stood at attention.

"Optios Wang, Chambers, and Brooke, I figured I'd find you here," the decurion said. "You have new orders." He handed them each a piece of sealed paper. Ethan ripped off the seal and opened it. The decurion spoke again.

"The Legion is mustering all off-duty personnel. You are to make your way to the nearest spaceport and report for duty no later than 12 hours from now."

"That's not a lot of time..." Julian said, frowning.

"It's not. So I suggest you all get moving."

"Yes sir."

The decurion left, probably on his way to the next watering hole to pick up more legionnaires.

"Well guys, that sort of ruined the evening," Ariel said. Julian grinned back at her.

"I guess it did... On the other hand, I think I'm just about ready to get out of here." Ethan didn't say anything. He felt ready as well, but guilty because he did. He knew Elsie would be heartbroken again, and he didn't look forward to it. There would definitely be tears tonight. He took one last swig from his beer before saying goodbye to the others. Then he stepped out and began walking home.

3.

The spaceport was crowded as ever, and Ethan, Ariel and Julian pushed their way through toward gate 38, where their LEO plane would be waiting. As soon as they saw the gate, Ethan noticed a redheaded legionnaire standing with her back toward them, talking to a group of others. His heart beat faster and he felt a familiar tingle, and at the same time he dreaded meeting this particular redhead. He had hoped to see Malika once he returned to Earth, but she was apparently still stationed at Mars. Instead here was the other woman in his life, Eileen. Remembering their passionate encounters during basic training made him flush.

The first to notice their approach, however, was another familiar face.

"Hey guys! Long time!" Antonio Avila, the Brazilian navy veteran become legionnaire smiled at them. After basic he'd been sent off to cavalry training, as had Eileen. He was wearing the big O signifying his new rank of Optio.

"So, they're mixing heavy infantry and cavalry for this one," Ariel said.

"Well, I think it's more like mixing all kinds. We're supposed to be the experienced troops by now," Antonio replied, indicating a group of legionnaires that had to be completely green. Like basic training green.

"Seriously?" Ethan said and trailed off. Antonio nodded, and filled them in on the latest news.

"The entire Legion is being reorganized. With the fresh meat we'll be ten full cohorts like before, but instead of being specialized like before, they will all be a mix of light and heavy infantry, cavalry, artillery and all kinds of auxiliaries. I guess Titan revealed that the old organization didn't work as well as it should have. I don't think they're done yet though."

"Yeah, Titan was..." Ariel never finished. No one spoke for a moment and Antonio's eyes grew wide.

"What, you were there?" He exclaimed. Ethan and the others kept silent. Ariel's face grew red; she obviously knew she had slipped.

"But, I thought no one survived... That the Lumins wiped out two full cohorts..." That was the official story, the one relayed through the official channels.

7

"Well, we survived." Ariel said in a low voice.

"A handful of us survived, that's all we can tell you," Ethan filled in, "and yeah, it was hell. Now, please, it's all classified, so if you wouldn't mind..."

Eileen, up until now quiet and distant, threw her arms around him, and hugged him tightly.

"We never knew... I'm glad you made it," she said as she loosed her grip on him. Ethan sighed.

"Too many good men and women died that day. I'm just hoping they'll let us pay the Lumins back, one way or another."

They continued catching up for a while, until the time came to board the LEO plane. Ethan found a seat, and Eileen quickly found one next to him, snuggling up to him.

"Maybe we'll find some time to ourselves, once we get wherever we're going," she whispered huskily into his ear. Ethan considered telling her about Malika, since she obviously didn't know, but he just couldn't find the words. Besides, who knew if Malika was even interested anymore. Not to mention the fact that they might be going into combat anytime. And besides, Eileen could be very persuasive.

The LEO plane took them straight to the edge of the atmosphere, shaking and shuddering all the way except for a few short minutes of weightlessness. It was all familiar to Ethan now, but as he craned over to see behind him, he saw Ariel, mouth tight and face white. How curious, that his friend, one of the bravest people he'd ever known, was so uncomfortable with flying.

Soon they were approaching the runway of another spaceport. They still didn't know where they were, but as soon as the hatch opened Ethan felt the hot, humid air of the tropics. He looked around. It was a different place from the one where he'd flown the last time around. He could see the ocean to the west and south, while jungle covered the east and north, except for a few large buildings that were obviously part of the spaceport itself. A senior decurion stepped up to them.

"Listen up. You won't be staying here for long, so I want you to remain in the closest building, or just outside it if you want. Your shuttle should arrive within the hour, and your departure is scheduled in three hours. As there are no officers present I want all NCOs to report to me if there's anything you need, or if you have any questions."

They settled in and Ethan kept wondering where they would be sent next. But no matter where they ended up, it couldn't be worse than Titan.

4.

Less than three hours later they were in the air again, this time pushing upward fast. Ethan felt like he was permanently stuck into his seat, and could barely move his arms. He slowly moved his head to the side. Eileen had grabbed a seat next to him once more, and smiled as their eyes met.

"Shit, I hate this part," he forced out. Eileen just stared back at him, but she didn't say anything. She looked as white as he felt. Even her flirtation had ceased, which Ethan thought spoke volumes.

Then, a few minutes later, they exited Earth's gravity well, and everything became easier, even breathing. The shuttle had an artificial gravity engine, but it only produced about fifty percent of Earth gravity, enough to feel familiar, but not enough to emulate what they were used to. Ethan was happy enough though.

Half an hour of Eileen's flirting later they docked with the starship.

The Excelsior was big enough to hold three full cohorts, but from what they had been told only one would occupy it. As soon as they entered through the airlock, they were led to a great staging area, and assigned to groups. Julian, a tech specialist, was singled out and left with another group, while the rest remained together. A huge screen showed a Tribune, a dark woman of perhaps fifty, with a stern look on her scarred face, wearing a simple olive legionnaire uniform. Contrary to the few higher ranking officers Ethan had seen before, she wore no distinctions other than her rank. She looked like a seasoned officer though; she just didn't flaunt it.

"Legionnaires!" She said, her loud voice amplified and echoing through the hold.

"You are to form the First Cohort of the Ghost Legion. I am your commander, Tribune Falck, and I expect nothing but the best from you." She paused as she looked out at the troops assembled before her.

"Now, you will be assigned to your units in a minute. Your orders will appear on your wrist pads, and you are to proceed and report to your units immediately. Training will commence shortly." She paused again.

"She looks like a tough one," Ariel whispered. Ethan couldn't agree more. He only hoped she was also smart, and that her subordinate officers were of the same quality.

"Our mission is to secure our mining operation on a rock called Ceres. Located in the asteroid belt between Mars and Jupiter, this is an important source of certain minerals, vital to our weapons manufacturing and, as such, a vital part of the war against the Lumins. The Lumins have established a foothold on the far side of the asteroid, but so far the mining operation has managed to continue, because of the heroic effort of the local defense force. However, intel informs us that an attack is imminent and that reinforcements may arrive at the enemy's base at any time. Our mission then, is two-fold. First, we are to secure the running operation of the mining facility, and make sure the enemy doesn't overrun it. Second, once we have a good defensive position, we are to take the initiative, and force the enemy to withdraw. If they don't, our final objective is to eliminate their presence. That means we'll slaughter them all." That last part was followed by a grin that told Ethan everything he needed to know about what his commander really wanted.

His wrist pad buzzed and he looked down. Beside him every legionnaire did the same. He parted from his friends and quickly made his way to the assigned area, where he presented himself to a centurion.

"Sir, Optio Wang reporting for duty." The centurion, a gray bearded man with ice blue eyes looked him up and down.

"Optio Wang, yes... Centurion Farrow here. I read your file. You're one of the survivors from Titan. Good, now report to Decurion Carr over there for further details." Dismissing him, the centurion turned away to speak to someone else. Ethan looked over to where he had indicated and saw a dark skinned, short, stocky woman who carried the D insignia. He made his way over and presented himself. The decurion didn't waste any time.

"Optio, I want you to head up one of my fire teams. Our squad is made up of four teams, with a heavy trooper leading each of them. You will lead two light troopers, whose mission will be to protect you and your weapon, carry as much ammo as they can, and generally keep you in business at any cost. Now," she paused and looked over at the other legionnaires gathered around her. She lowered her voice. "The lighties are green. I mean, really green. That's how we've managed to get back to full strength, at least numbers-wise, after Titan. So you drive them hard, and make sure they get up to speed as soon as possible. You have little more than a week before we land on Ceres, so make it count."

"Yes ma'am," Ethan replied.

5.

The journey was meant to last a little more than a week, and Ethan made sure his fire team spent every available hour preparing for the mission. When they didn´t spend time getting familiar with each other, training with the rest of the squad, or the platoon, Ethan had them doing physical training, or rehearsing dropship routines and emergency procedures.

The legionnaires on his team were Gavin Samson, an American farmer´s son from the Mid-West and Helena Neuwijnkel, a blonde Dutch city girl that had joined up as soon as she finished school. Both were eager, and relatively competent, but Ethan worked them hard to wean out bad habits and ineffective practices.

"Optio, sir..." Helena began, but Ethan cut her off.

"Don´t sir me, Legionnaire. I work for a living."

"I´m sorry, Optio..."

"Look, I´m not an officer. Barely an NCO. It´s just the three of us, so just call me Ethan."

"Ethan, do you know anything about the strength of the enemy?"

"Well, I don´t know any more than you do, but listen, the locals have managed to hold them off so far, so the Lumins cannot be very strong. For now. However, we should be expecting them to be reinforced at any time. We don´t have a strong hold on the asteroid belt, so they should be able to ship in reinforcements if they wanted to. Besides, Ceres is an important source of raw materials for our weapons production, which the Lumins surely want as well. In any case, they´d want to deny us the resources. Not to mention that Ceres is strategically important in itself, being the largest object in the belt." Gavin and Helena were nodding now, and Ethan appreciated the fact that they were paying close attention. Gavin, normally not one to speak up, did for a change.

"So if the Lumins take Ceres they may even use it for a staging platform to attack the inner planets and moons?"

"That's right. The other asteroids are too small to make much of a difference, other than the resources mined. In fact, the Lumins already hold a few of them. But losing Ceres would be a huge blow to human defense."

Decurion Carr spent quite a bit of time with them as well, both with the individual fire teams and the squad as a whole. She introduced Ethan to the other optios, the specialists leading each of the other fire teams. She lead one team herself, and she made it clear she expected the optios to follow her example, follow suit, and make their teams behave as both individual fighting units, but also as parts of the squad.

Optio Sharon, an Israeli veteran of the IDF, was the oldest member of the squad, and a host of knowledge, having fought wars most of his life, first for his country and later for all of humanity. A veteran of the Lumin War, he'd been cast aside afterward, and his story reminded Ethan of the one told by Senior Decurion Ford, the man who recruited him to the Legion.

"Optio Sharon is the kind of soldier who gets recommended for promotion all the time, and then he goes and does something stupid outside of duty. The man should have been a Senior Decurion by now, perhaps even an officer." Decurion Carr gave him a look that seemed a mix between admonition and fondness before she continued.

"When it comes to warfare, you will learn well by listening to him, but do not, I repeat, do not let him give you any marriage advice, and if you ever see him when on leave, run as far as you can."

The grizzled veteran chuckled at the decurion's words, shook his head, and winked at Ethan.

"Don't listen to her. I'm just a foot soldier, that's all," he said.

Decurion Carr snorted and introduced the other optio.

"Optio Warren here, however..." She pointed at a tall woman with short-cropped blonde hair. "Now here's a future officer for you. A reliable soldier, a good leader, and well liked even by the brass. Now, she doesn't have combat experience, having lucked out of the Titan disaster, but once she does I'm sure she'll have a squad of her own in no time."

On the tenth day, everyone was told to gear up, and get ready to drop. Adjunct Levinson, Ethan's platoon commander, personally stood beside the hatch leading into the airlock to their dropship, patting each soldier on the back, and giving them approving nods and encouragement, as they entered the ship. Ethan liked him, even if he hadn't spoken more than a few

15

words to him, and smiled back as he entered the dropship. He took a seat and strapped in. Tribune Falck's voice came on the loudspeakers.

"Legionnaires. We have orbited Ceres for the last 12 hours, scouting the ground, and the first elements of the cohort will be dropped in less than five minutes. You will land inside the defensive perimeter of the Ernutet crater, where the human colony is located. Your officers have all been briefed on your individual assignments, and you are to form up and get to your destinations as quickly as possible. We expect this to be a cold drop, as there has been no sign of hostilities for the last week. Nevertheless, be vigilant, prepare for the worst, and pay attention to your officers at all times. The locals have been instructed to remain in position, so there will be no welcoming committee. They have done a good job at protecting the colony so far, but now it's our turn, and they have agreed to stay out of the way. Best of luck to you."

The loudspeaker clicked and the sound was replaced by the clangs and clicks of the dropship beginning launch procedures.

"Legionnaires, visors down, perform final checks," Adjunct Levinson shouted.

A few minutes later they were speeding down toward the surface of Ceres.

6.

As soon as the dropship landed, the main hatch opened. Not slowly and controlled as it sometimes did during exercises and training, but shooting outward, landing hard on the ground below, accompanied by clangs and bangs, strangely muffled by the thin atmosphere at the landing zone.

"Go, go, go," the adjunct shouted, with decurions and optios repeating his words down the chain of command. Ethan stormed out, his heavy machine gun hanging from his carrying harness, ready to fire at any time. He also carried a rocket launcher on his back, while his team members carried a heavy load of ammo for the machine gun and several rockets each. At least, it would have been heavy in Earth gravity. Here on Ceres it was nothing. They could have carried twice as much without weight being an issue.

As soon as they were out, they ran to their position, and lay low, waiting for further orders.

"Third squad follow me," Decurion Carr shouted, and Ethan got up and began moving out, still ready to fire at anything.

The perimeter looked empty at first, but then Ethan started noticing movement here and there. Carefully hidden locals, peering out from their hideouts.

"It's like they're afraid of us," Helena said.

"No," Ethan replied. "They've been told to stay out of the way, so we can get into position as quickly as possible. We're taking over the defense of this place and it has to happen as quickly and smoothly as possible, so it doesn't give the Lumins a chance to attack during the transition."

They moved quickly to their predetermined spots, and set up the heavy machine gun nest first. Helena laid out the ammo storage and made sure the gun could be easily reloaded without the loader being exposed to direct fire. In the meantime Ethan and Gavin set up the rocket launcher position next to the machine gun. This was hidden from view, so the enemy wouldn't know they had the capability. Spare rockets were laid out in a metal crate next to the launcher position, to allow for easy access.

As soon as the weapons were up and ready, they began checking the fire zone and line-of-sight comms to the rest of the squad. A few spots had to be smoothed out to deny the enemy any form of easy cover, but otherwise they soon had a good defensive position, with a clear line of fire and good line-of-sight to either side. When Decurion Carr came to check up on them she gave them a satisfied nod. Then she spoke into her helmet,

"Sir, third squad is in position and ready."

7.

The living quarters of the small colony was laid out underground, in tunnels and dug out caverns, and the legionnaires were given four and six- man rooms to share, in newly dug out areas deep beneath where the miners and their families lived. The rooms were never full, as a number of them were always on guard duty or as part of the quick response reserve, who stayed up top. Eileen and Antonio and the rest of the cavalry detachment were the core of the reserve, while the infantry rotated on a fixed schedule.

Two weeks after landing Ethan found himself alone in his room, having completed an eight-hour shift outside, followed by four hours in reserve. Eileen had been on the same reserve team as him and although she had kept things professional, she had definitely been flirting. Ethan thought he might have to speak with her about it. They didn't have time for this; not here, and he still hadn't said anything about Malika to her.

He removed his suit and laid it aside next to his helmet. Then he checked his sidearm, a special pistol carried by heavy infantry; heavy caliber, low mag capacity, and meant as a last resort only. He removed his holster and laid it aside as well. Then he dimmed the lights and crept into bed, falling asleep within seconds.

He awoke to the sound of breathing next to his ear, and immediately scrambled for the gun.

"Hush, it's me," he heard a familiar whisper. Eileen. She opened his sleeping bag, and snuggled in beside him. She was naked. Ethan wondered how she had managed to undress and come this close without his noticing. Her hands interrupted his thoughts, as they slid across his body, then down.

"Eileen, this is..." he began, but she quieted him with a kiss. Then another, and his resistance melted away.

They made love like they had never done back in basic training. It was more intense, and once Ethan's hesitation faded, so did his inhibitions. At one point her

19

moans became so loud a guard, one of the locals, came running.

"Go away!" Eileen groaned, and the flustered guard got out as fast as he could, muttering apologies.

They climaxed together, and lay in each other's arms for a long time afterward.

"Don't worry, Ethan," Eileen said once she got up and began dressing. "I won't tell her." Ethan stared at her. She just laughed softly.

"Malika, Ethan. Of course I know. Remember what I told you before, I'm not yours and you're not mine. Doesn't mean we can't have some fun from time to time, right? Well, if you love her, really love her, I guess we can't... But we're young, and I hope you didn't make any promises." Ethan didn't know what to say, so he stayed quiet. Eileen seemed to take that as tacit agreement, and smiled before she gave him a quick kiss.

"You have two hours before your next shift, so better get some sleep," she said and walked out.

8.

Ethan avoided Eileen the next few days, which passed quickly. Three weeks after their arrival, another starship arrived in orbit, and soon after several landers - about four times the size of a dropship, began delivering materiel and personnel. One of the first of the newcomers Ethan noticed was Optio Morales, who had been an instructor during basic training before leaving for cavalry training with Eileen and Antonio. Now a decurion, she commanded a Behemoth, a heavily armored tracked vehicle, similar to the main battle tanks of the past, but equipped with a more versatile arsenal instead of the traditional cannon. All of them were built to deliver overwhelming firepower at high speed though, a cavalry tactic as ancient as the horseman. Ethan had never become casual around Morales, so he just watched as the column of six behemoths passed them, and headed out of the perimeter.

"Dec, do you know what that's all about?" he asked Decurion Carr on the comms.

"They're doing a sweep of the area between us and the last known Lumin sighting. That's all I've been told. Glad to have them though. From what I hear, the behemoth crews are the only seasoned troops in this latest batch. The rest are all green, straight outta basic."

Three hours later the behemoths returned without incident, and not long after Ethan and his team rotated out to get some rest.

A familiar face stood just inside the living quarters.

"Ethan, I should say Optio Wang now. I saw you earlier when we rode out, so I figured I'd come by and say hi," the man said.

"Tom, what are you doing here? I thought they kicked you out," Ethan exclaimed, not sure what to say. Tom Lowry had washed out of basic training during the final mountain run, and Ethan had figured he'd washed out of the Legion entirely. Tom laughed softly.

"I had to go through all of basic again, only this time I made it. I was going through cavalry training when they pulled me out. They sent me off to the spaceport with a bunch of others, and here I am. I only had about a week left to go, so I guess they figured I'd be all right."

"Tom, it's really good to see you! I'm sorry that Jamila isn't here to see you, last I heard she was on Mars." Tom nodded somberly.

"Well, who knows how things are between us now anyway. But let's not think about that right now." Ethan nodded and moved to include Helena and Gavin, who had been standing behind him.

"Helena and Gavin, this is Tom Lowry. Helena and Gavin are part of my fire team. Tom, you're... doing what exactly?" He realized he didn't know what Tom did, other than that he was part of the behemoth crew.

"I'm a gunner. Well, I guess it's almost like a tech job. I just run a bunch of computers; most of the time my job is to make sure the AI does what we want it to, but sometimes I fire semi- manually, or SM as we call it. Means I choose the targets, decide when to fire, switch up the AI's priorities and such."

Ethan nodded slowly. He didn't know much of how the behemoths operated, but he figured some of it might be compared to using the exoskeletons, where AIs ran several systems, including self-defense systems that caught threats that the human senses might overlook.

"Well, how about we get something to eat, and we can talk shop over dinner," Ethan said, smiling. The four legionnaires walked down to the mess hall together.

9.

Two days later, the alarms began blaring, and Ethan stormed up and out, along with the rest of his squad, who were all off duty. They quickly got to their positions on the western side, Ethan manning the heavy machine gun, with Helena and Gavin on either side with their heavy assault rifles, ready to assist Ethan and defend their position.

"We have heavy incoming from the east," Decurion Carr's voice spoke inside the helmet comms. "We're to stay put here for now, in case there's another attack as well. Looks like the infantry will hold them off, but the response team is getting ready to move out there to bolster their defense."

Ethan looked around. So far this area was quiet, but that could change at any time, so his hands never left the machine gun.

"Gavin, if we're ordered to move out, you are to take the rocket launcher. Helena, you carry as much ammo and rockets as you can."

Ceres didn't have a stable atmosphere, but every now and then enough water vapor escaped from the ground through cracks and vents, causing a brief period where an unstable atmosphere formed, until it dissipated again soon after. In that time, sound could carry across the barren landscape, usually in the form of distorted noise from behemoths and other machinery. The sound was weak, but it was there, until the atmosphere dissipated and Ceres became quiet again.

Right now, Ethan was able to hear the rumble of behemoths starting up, and he turned to watch as they rolled across the perimeter, toward where the enemy had attacked. He noticed that there was no air power attacking the Lumins, which struck him as odd. Well, he'd seen how the dropships had been easy targets for the Lumin mech droids back on Titan, but he'd expect the Legion to be able to come up with a solution in order to give air support to the troops on the ground. But clearly, the Legion brass had decided the ground forces would have to do by themselves this time around.

The behemoths would give the mech droids a real fight though. Their heavy, reactive armor, could withstand even direct hits from some pretty nasty weaponry, and when they returned fire it would be overwhelming, each behemoth able to fire several weapons systems simultaneously.

True enough, moments later the sound of battle amplified tenfold, as the behemoths let loose on the attacking Lumins.

A few minutes later the noise died down, and Ethan couldn't tell if it was the atmosphere dissipating or that the behemoths were rolling over the attackers, away from the perimeter. Decurion Carr interrupted his thoughts.

"Third squad, on me. We have a new mission. The locals are taking over our positions."

10.

As soon as the squad had gathered, Decurion Carr led them inside the building where the response team would normally be located. As soon as the airlock closed, she removed her helmet. Other squads were standing around as well, while some moved on to the lower levels, to get their briefings down there.

"Right, let's see if we can get this piece of crap to work..." She fiddled with a remote, and a giant screen on the wall lit up. The first thing Ethan noticed were images of approaching mech droids. He shuddered, memories of Titan resurfacing for a moment.

"This is the feed from the first wave. Mech droids, like the ones who took out two cohorts on Titan. Not many though, but enough to breach the defense line until the response team came and plugged the hole." Ethan hadn't known that the Lumins had been this close to overrunning the perimeter, but he knew enough to pay close attention.

"Now, just like on Titan, the Lumins seem to have adopted new tactics, where they send these mech droids out to fight in their stead. However, we did observe this," she said, and flicked to a new feed, showing a blurry image of something huge, advancing on the poor legionnaires doing the filming. The feed only lasted for a few seconds, before the screen went blank.

"These were the only images we got before the behemoths joined the fighting."

"Decurion, " Optio Sharon interrupted. The decurion let him speak. "What is that huge thing in the last feed?" Decurion Carr grinned, clearly expecting the question.

"That is a Lumin. Or rather, that is an exoskeleton with a Lumin inside. It seems they don't leave all the fighting to their machines after all. So, we're facing a combined force of mech droids and Lumin heavy infantry, and here's the good part; the brass have decided that our cohort is going to take them out, once and for all."

No one spoke. They were soldiers, ready to take the fight to the enemy if ordered to, but everyone knew what had happened the last time Humans and Lumins had clashed. Titan.

"Why don't we just bomb the shit out of them from orbit?" Optio Warren asked. The decurion flicked a switch on her remote, and the screen changed to a view of a grey, metallic background.

"I'll let someone else answer that."

The face of Tribune Tanner appeared, and Ethan was reminded of his own initiation into the Legion. Jeremy Tanner had been a half-crazy test administrator who had told Ethan that he'd never become a regular soldier, in between singing and repeating himself over and over again. Only after Ethan and the few survivors of Titan had returned to their starships had he learned that Jeremy Tanner was a tribune in the Legion, and something of an actor. His true role seemed to be that of an intelligence operator, and Ethan suspected he had a lot to do with the strategic choices being made here on Ceres. The tribune smiled before he spoke.

26

"Legionnaires, today we are going to kick the Lumins out of the asteroid belt."

11.

Ethan lowered his visor as he prepared for descent. The ship was high enough for the legionnaires to feel almost weightless, almost high enough to enter a low orbit. Ethan thought back on the briefing, and how Tribune Tanner had laid out the plan to them. Optio Warren had asked why they didn't just bomb the Lumins from orbit, and he had chuckled.

"Their shields protect them from anything we could throw at them from above, barring nukes, which we won't use, due to the valuable minerals in the ground. However, as we speak, the behemoths are paving their way into the Lumin stronghold. We expect to lose a few of them, but we hope that enough will be able to get through so they can knock out part of the lower shielding capacity. That way, their shields may protect the Lumins from above, but not from a ground attack."

"Now, the dropships will land just behind the protection of the behemoths, which will support your attack. Each dropship will carry a platoon of infantry, along with a tech detachment. Your mission is to take out the mech droids and the Lumins controlling them. The tech detachments have their own orders, and you will protect them and make sure they get access to everything. We think we're approaching a breakthrough

27

here, and the survival of the techs and their data is vital."

The dropship shook less than Ethan was used to because of the thin to non-existent atmosphere of Ceres, but nevertheless, he felt the drag of their descent.

A robot voice began counting down the last few seconds.

"Ten," the voice began, and Ethan closed his eyes. He was ready, so all that remained was to wait.

"Nine, eight, seven, six."

His stomach knotted, remembering the last time he'd dropped into combat. Almost everyone who had dropped with him was dead now.

"Five, four, three."

He opened his eyes and looked around, wondering how many of the legionnaires around him would be alive at the end of the day.

"Two, one, zero."

The dropship bounced, and settled. The hatch flung open. An explosion nearby rocked the ship as Ethan exited through the hatch, and he nearly lost his footing. He looked around.

"Third squad on me," he heard Decurion Carr's voice, and knew she'd be to his right. He ran over, followed by Helena and Gavin, as the dropship took off and got out from harm's way.

In front of them they could see the behemoths fighting several mech droids and a few Lumins in exoskeletons. One behemoth was reduced to rubble, while another was burning. No sign of the crew though. That was a bad sign.

"Second platoon, advance!" That was adjunct Levinson. The squads immediately began moving forward, keeping the behemoths between themselves and the enemy.

"We'll move in between that hulk at two o'clock and the one still firing at three," Decurion Carr said. Ethan made sure he had Helena and Gavin close by. A mech droid who managed to pass the burning behemoth began firing at the infantry, tearing them up fast.

"Third squad, take out that mech droid. Quickly, before it takes out the entire platoon!" Decurion Carr had seen what was happening and Ethan knew that they only had a few seconds. He turned his machine gun toward the mech droid and fired a short burst, adjusted his sighting and then he emptied an entire box of ammo.

He dropped to a knee, and removed the carrying harness attached to the gun.

"Helena, switch barrels. Gavin, give me the rocket launcher." Helena took the machine gun and began switching the scorching hot barrel. Gavin handed him the rocket launcher, and Ethan took aim and fired. The rocket hit the mech droid, and he could see parts exploding. Incredibly, the mech droid, still standing, was still able to fire at the legionnaires nearby.

"Gavin, feed me!" Gavin inserted another rocket, and Ethan fired again.

This time the mech droid dropped forward, having lost a limb and probably its ability to sight as well. The legionnaires closer to it finished it off, as Ethan got back into the carrying harness with the machine gun, while handing over the rocket launcher to Gavin.

"Nice work," the adjunct said on the platoon channel. "Whoever took out that beast, I'm putting you on my list for promotion."

Ethan chuckled. He'd heard that one before.

12.

Once the legionnaires broke through the Lumin defenses, the enemy didn't last long. Ethan's century was the first inside the enemy compound, and soon the area was secured. The techs went to work, bringing out all sorts of samples, data archives and equipment, and loaded into a waiting transport. Ethan looked for Julian, who he knew was with the tech detachment, but he couldn't find him.

Ethan's platoon had avoided casualties altogether, even though there were a few minor wounds here and there; nothing the medics couldn't handle. Helena had burned her hands when switching barrels on the heavy machine gun, as had a couple others in the squad. A common enough injury that happened during training and combat alike. They were soon patched up with synth-skin, and good to go.

Ethan watched as Decurion Morales passed by. She nodded slightly, and Ethan nodded back. It wasn't that they didn't like each other; they just had never grown close, not like he had with NCOs like Walker, Schwartz, Blake or even Trudeau. Perhaps that might change, now that they'd seen combat together. She

30

looked worn though, and no wonder; the cavalry had taken the heaviest casualties, protecting the infantry. If Ethan were to guess, he'd say almost half the behemoths had been taken out.

He looked around and saw Tom Lowry sat slumped beside a medic. His head was covered by a first aid survival tent, which was basically just a plastic bag filled with air, and an oxygen supply hose attached to a tank. It could save a man in this environment, if he was recovered quickly. It seemed Tom had been lucky. His uniform was torn and burnt though, and now that he noticed he saw that Tom's face looked like it had been badly burnt as well, with blisters covering most of his left cheek. He stepped over to him.

"Hey man, what happened?" Ethan said. Tom slowly turned his head to look up at him. It was obvious he'd been crying, but now his eyes were empty, his pupils like little pinpricks. His words came out slurred, but coherent.

"Ethan, I should have died back there. My entire crew... We took a hit, and... And everything caught fire. I got out through the escape hatch before the entire... every one of them..."

"Optio, please, he needs to rest," the medic next to Tom said, and Ethan nodded. He moved as if to give his friend a pat on the shoulder, but stopped. He didn't know if Tom had burns there, or how he'd react. So he took a step back and saw Decurion Carr waving him over. He turned and walked over to his superior.

"Optio Wang, that was one hell of a performance. Adjunct Levinson noticed as well. He asked around, and

I told him you were the one who took out that mech droid. You saved a lot of lives today."

"Thank you ma'am," Ethan said. "So, do you think this will help kick the Lumins out of the belt?"

"I sure hope so. Anyway, there's a transport coming to pick us up in fifteen minutes, so we'd better pack up and move out of here."

13.

The list of casualties was released later that evening. Ethan looked long and hard until he found the name he'd been searching for. Believing it because you couldn't find someone wherever you looked was one thing, but seeing the name among the confirmed dead was another. It didn't make him cry, as he'd expected. It made him feel empty, as if he'd lost a part of himself. He hadn't loved her, not like that, but she'd been special to him, and someone he'd considered close. Very close.

Eileen Green had been his first. Now she was dead; cooked inside her burning behemoth along with her crew. Ethan couldn't imagine a worse fate. Burned alive until there was nothing left, the heat so all-consuming that not even the bones remained. The only consolation he could find was that it had probably happened so fast she might not even have felt much before the crew was incinerated.

"I'm sorry son," someone said from behind him. Ethan turned and saw the last person he'd expected; Tribune Jeremy Tanner. "I know she was your friend."

"The cavalry paid a high price," Ethan said. The tribune nodded.

"Yes, they did. And they saved a lot of infantry lives. Without their sacrifice most of you would be dead, and we'd be nowhere closer to chasing the Lumins out of the belt."

"You think it's a fair price?"

"I do. Harsh, but fair."

The two men stood staring at each other for a moment, quietly waiting for the other so say something. In the end, Tribune Tanner pulled out a small black box from his pocket and handed it to Ethan.

"Here, open it."

Ethan took it and opened the lid. Inside were two black Ds.

"You've earned these," the tribune said. Ethan didn't know what to say, so he took one out. Tribune Tanner reached out and took it from his hand, fastened it to his lapel. Then he did the same with the other one.

"Congratulations, Decurion Wang." He extended his hand, and Ethan took it.

Tribune Tanner turned to walk away, but Ethan had a question he'd been pondering ever since he joined the Legion.

"Wait, sir. There's something I was never able to figure out. You were there right at the beginning, at the Recruitment Office. You told me I'd be rejected everywhere, which turned out to be true, and yet, the Legion took me in at once. Hell, sir, I've been promoted twice now, so I think I'm doing pretty well as a soldier. I don't get it sir. None of it makes any sense to me." Tribune Tanner smiled and tapped his nose twice.

"Classified, son," he said, but Ethan wouldn't take it. Not today.

"Sir, I think I have a right to know. I just lost a good friend today, and I have to know. Why did the Legion want a reject like me? Heck, three rejects if you count Optio Chambers and Optio Brooke, and they seem to be doing all right as well!" Ethan stopped, realizing his voice had risen almost to a shout, and people around were looking. He could get demoted or worse for this kind of behavior.

Tribune Tanner didn't say anything. His eyes had a darkness to them that Ethan hadn't noticed before. When he spoke, his words came clipped, in a way that made it clear that it would be his final answer.

"I'll give you the answer, although you may not like it, Decurion. Afterward, you are not to speak of it again, not to a living soul. The truth is, I control the selections. Whenever I notice a potential recruit that would be a good fit for the Legion, I make sure he or she is given a poor rating. In fact, if they really have potential, the kind I saw in you, I make sure you won't even get a job waiting tables or digging radioactive mud in civilian life as well. Just to make sure. So in your case, whether you took that first contract or not, you would eventually have found your way back to the basement of the Recruitment Office, where I'd be waiting."

"So I never had a choice?" Ethan whispered. Tribune Tanner nodded slowly.

"You didn't. Now, most legionnaires have volunteered more freely, just so we're clear. In fact you wanted to serve, didn't you? I just led you in the right direction." And with that, he turned on his heel and walked away.

Part 2

14.

When Ethan returned to his quarters, Helena and Gavin were already asleep, so he tried not to wake them up. Antonio sat on a bunk, obviously waiting for him. When Ethan entered, he got up and embraced him.

"I'm sorry about Eileen," he said. "I know how much she meant to you, and I know you meant a lot to her as well. More than she let on, I can tell you that much." Ethan felt a pressure in his chest, and tears building up in the corner of his eye. He forced it back down as they let go of the embrace.

"Yeah, I..." Ethan couldn't finish, so he just shook his head.

"Tom 's hurt as well," he said, changing the subject slightly.

"He'll be alright though, he was lucky."

"Yeah..."

"What's that on your lapels? Shit man, you got the D!" Antonio's voice had risen, and Ethan tried to get him to be silent, but it was too late. Helena and Gavin both got up from their bunks, rubbing sleep out of their eyes.

"Congrats man," Antonio said, and slapped his shoulder.

"Thanks..."

"I guess you'll be heading a squad now, or something," Gavin added as he got up to congratulate Ethan. Helena was last and surprised him by giving him a kiss on the cheek.

36

"Hey! Now I want a promotion too!" Antonio grinned. Helena grinned back at him and kissed Ethan again, this time on the other cheek.

"Hey hey, now this is very unprofessional," Ethan said, half joking. Helena was an attractive young woman, but she was a green legionnaire and he was her superior. He hadn't avoided seeing her shapely form, and she had a really sexy way of swaying her hips when she walked. But it was look but never touch as far as Ethan was concerned. He turned and saw Decurion Carr enter as well.

"I told you," she just said, smiling, as she walked up to him. Being a head shorter, she looked up at him, obviously pleased with his promotion. When Ethan didn't reply, she shook her head.

"I know, I know, you're sad because your friend died, so you don't want no fuss about that damn promotion, I get it." The woman grabbed him by the neck and pulled him down, planting a big kiss on Ethan's mouth.

"Still, I think you've earned it. Congratulations," she said.

"Whoa!" Antonio exclaimed. Ethan pulled back, surprised.

"Hell yeah, that's how we do it where I'm from," Decurion Carr said, planting her hands on her wide hips. "Now that we're all done kissing and weeping and congratulating, we've got work to do. Decurion Wang, if you don't mind, follow me. We've got new orders, and all NCOs and officers are to attend the briefing in five minutes." She turned toward the others. "You all, get

37

back to whatever you were doing. Optio Avila, get the hell out of this room, my soldiers need their beauty sleep, got it?" Antonio straightened and saluted her.

"Yes Ma'am." Ethan and Decurion Carr turned to leave, but Antonio coughed.

"Ah, Decurion," he said. Both turned back toward him.

"Not you Ethan, ah, Decurion Carr, just one question, and please don't take this the wrong way. If I ever get promoted, will you kiss me as well?" he asked. Ethan's jaw dropped. What the hell was his friend thinking? Decurion Carr though, just walked back up to Antonio, until she stood just a few centimeters away, looking up at him.

"If you ever get promoted," she whispered, loud enough for everyone to hear, "I promise I'll kiss you, Optio Avila. I might even ask you out on a real date. But until then, if I hear one more word from you, I'll kick your ass so hard you won't sit for a week. Got it?"

Antonio nodded, wide eyed. It was obvious he didn't dare open his mouth, from fear of what might come out.

15.

The meeting didn't last long, and Ethan was glad when Tribune Falck dismissed them. The entire cohort would be going to Mars, where they would reinforce the three cohorts already stationed there. He didn't know how he felt about the possibility of running into Malika again, but he figured he'd just have to deal with it somehow. His quick exit was interrupted by the booming voice of his commanding officer though.

"First Century on me", Centurion Farrow bellowed above the noise and chatter of exiting NCOs and officers. Ethan and the rest of the officers and NCOs from the First gathered in a wide circle around the bearded commander.

"There will be a few minor adjustments, and I thought we'd take care of it now as opposed to in transit. Adjunct DeBeers, you lost an experienced squad leader, so I'm giving you Decurion Carr from Second Platoon. Adjunct Levinson, you have a newly promoted decurion in your platoon, Wang, who will replace Carr. As soon as possible after we land on Mars we're going to shake things up again, so these adjustments are just for now. Also, we had a few hiccups with Third Platoon, so we're switching back to..." Ethan didn't follow the rest as he had enough on his mind. He hoped he was ready to command a squad. Thankfully, he had Optio Sharon, who had more experience than the rest of his squad altogether.

Soon after, transports began to lift the different units off Ceres. Ethan found he was looking forward to seeing Mars, which was one of the Legion's strongholds, housing at least three cohorts at any given time, and much of the Legion's command structure. Now that the Lumins on Ceres were beaten there would be mostly mopping up operations in the asteroid belt. He was glad to see that work being given to others. Mars, in comparison seemed like a holiday. As far as he knew, there were no Lumins on Mars.

"Sir, I need a heavy trooper to replace myself," he said as soon as he managed to speak to Adjunct Levinson, who commanded Second Platoon.

"I don't have any to spare, Decurion. I can give you a light trooper but that's it. You'll just have to improvise. I'm sure you'll figure something out."

Ethan had expected this answer, so he had already given it some thought. As soon as they boarded The Excelsior, he gathered his squad in one of the holds where they usually trained.

"We need to switch things up a bit, so here's what I've been thinking. Instead of four three-man teams we'll switch to three four-man teams. I'll lead one and Optios Sharon and Warren will take one each. Instead of one heavy gunner and two support, we'll each train one light trooper to man the rocket launchers, so in effect we get two heavies supported by two light troopers."

As soon as Ethan had laid out his plan and divided the squad into teams, they began rehearsing. The flight to Mars would take about a week, so they focused on getting a handle on minor tactical adjustments and training the lighties who would, in effect, become rocketeers. Ethan would man one heavy machine gun himself, with Helena for support, and Gavin was to man the rocket launcher. Gavin's supporting light trooper was a new guy called Erwin Rauch, a replacement pulled out of Third Platoon. A decent enough soldier, Ethan figured he'd do just fine.

16.

After two days of practicing the new squad setup, Optio Sharon pulled him aside.

"Decurion," he said, "I don't know why we haven't tried this before. This way we get so much more firepower, I mean, with the machine gun and rocket launcher working in concert like this. We should use this setup all over. And the light troopers, well, some of them might become heavies later, and this way we get to screen and evaluate as well."

"Thanks Optio, that means a lot coming from you," Ethan replied, honestly surprised and flattered.

"I'm telling you Dec, you'll become an officer one of these days. You have a talent."

Ethan smiled as Optio Levi Sharon walked off. He hadn't known how the grizzled veteran would react, taking orders from a man half his age. He was glad to have a man like Levi on his side.

He walked through the corridors, which were bustling with legionnaires, some fully donned in armor and a variety of weaponry, crew in their grey coveralls, and here and there a civilian. Ethan wondered for a moment what civilians were doing on a military vessel, but he figured it would be government officials or something like that. As he walked he kept thinking about how it would be if Malika was still stationed on Mars. If nothing else, they would eventually bump into each other. Had she waited, he though, and immediately felt guilty; he sure hadn't. Eileen's death didn't change anything in that regard.

He reached the area assigned to First Century. Ariel stood waiting for him, along with Adjunct Levinson and a decurion he didn't remember the name of.

"Decurion Wang, the adjunct said. The decurion standing beside him smiled broadly, and extended a hand. Ethan took it.

"I'm Decurion Snow," the man said in a British accent. "Optio Chambers here speaks highly of you. She says you've reorganized your squad a bit, that you've found a way to achieve greater firepower and better utilization of the light infantry."

"He's the guy," Ariel said.

"I'd love for you to explain this to me, as I'm in a similar situation. That is, lacking trained heavy infantry, which I hear is the situation in several units."

"If this works as well in the field as in theory, we might reorganize the entire platoon this way," Adjunct Levinson commented. "Decurion Wang seems to have a talent for this."

"Well sir, the legionnaires seem to find it works well enough," Ethan said.

"Splendid," Snow exclaimed. "Do you have time for a cup of tea, Decurion? Or perhaps coffee for you?"

"Sure," Ethan said, "just let me get out of my combat gear. He walked over to his bunk, situated next to those of the rest of his squad. The rest of them were coming in to clean up and get some rest, and he gave them all a few words of approval. "Sweat saves blood, Dec," Gavin replied. Ethan couldn't have agreed more.

A few minutes later Ethan and Decurion Snow found a place to sit in the recreational area nearby.

"Please, call me Ben," Decurion Snow said, "It's short for Benjamin, but only my mother calls me that."

"All right Ben, I'm Ethan."

The spent half an hour discussing tactics and squad setup, knowing there was a window of opportunity at this time, with the entire Legion being reorganized, when testing and experimentation were actively being welcomed.

"It hasn't always been like this," Ben explained. "There was a way of doing everything, the Legion way, they called it. And it seemed to work. I remember as a green legionnaire, some four years ago, I was assigned to an outpost in the belt. I had a few ideas, but even mentioning them was unthinkable. No officer would listen to a mere legionnaire. Even just a year ago, when I was promoted to Decurion, this was the way of things. Titan changed all that."

Ethan shot him a look.

"Don't worry, I know this is all classified, but I'm Optio Chamber's squad leader, remember. I'm privileged to read her service history, and adding two and two together, I'm guessing you were one of the survivors. A qualified guess, I suppose."

They looked at each other, and when Ethan said nothing to contradict his reasoning, Ben nodded to himself and took a sip of his tea.

"I guess losing two entire cohorts, more than a thousand legionnaires, would cause even the brass to reconsider things," Ethan finally said.

"Exactly. Sometimes it takes a tragedy to bring about change for the better."

"Well, let´s hope so."

17.

Mars, the red planet, looked just like Ethan had imagined; red dust everywhere and open landscapes in every direction. As soon as The Excelsior entered a stable orbit, transports began carrying soldiers and equipment down to the surface. Ethan and the rest of First Century was among the first to land on the Elysium Spaceport, followed by several dropships able to carry the entire century quickly into combat, if necessary. The Elysium province was Ghost Legion territory, whereas other legions and regular defense forces each had their separate areas of responsibility. North of the Elysium base was the largest volcano in the area, Elysium Mons, while the base itself was located on the Elysium Plains.

While the rest of the cohort was ferried down to the surface, First Century was moving into their quarters at Camp Elysium, east of the Spaceport. Almost three thousand strong once First Cohort settled in, the Mars detachment was the largest concentration of legionnaires anywhere, a force consisting of light and heavy infantry, cavalry, artillery and every kind of auxiliaries.

An adjunct led Ethan´s platoon to their barracks. The barracks were buried underneath the surface, protecting them from radiation, and they were surprisingly spacious and comfortable. Once inside, they removed their helmets and Centurion Farrow assigned each platoon to its part of the barracks, each squad to their separate rooms. As squad leader, Ethan assigned each legionnaire to his or her bunk.

"I could live here," one of the legionnaires exclaimed.

"Well, this is one of the better postings," the adjunct said, smiling.

"Sure beats Oxtaba," Optio Sharon murmured. The adjunct gave him a sideways look that spoke volumes. Ethan remembered some of the veteran legionnaires mentioning this Oxtaba on several occasions before, and made a mental note to ask Sharon about it one day. They all gathered in the common room, which was the only room big enough to hold the entire century.

"Please, can I have your attention," the adjunct said, loud enough for everyone to hear.

"There's a starship coming in three days, carrying an envoy from the Blue Sector Confederacy. When the envoy arrives those of you not tied up by other duties will be part of an honor guard to welcome this dignitary. You will be given further instructions later, so this is just an early warning." He paused for a moment, allowing the news to sink in. Ethan had never seen one of their allies of the Confederacy. In fact he hadn't seen much of their involvement at all. All he knew of them was that they had helped Earth during the invasion, and that Earth had become part of the Confederacy in the process.

"One last thing," the adjunct said. "Ten kilometers east of here is a small detachment of prisoners, criminals sentenced to forced labor here in the Elysium province. I want you to go no closer than two kilometers from the area - don't worry it is well marked on your maps - the prison guards are regular defense and not part of the Legion, and we'd like to avoid any sort of confusion or misunderstandings. They do tend to... frown upon anyone, especially armed personnel, coming too close to them. So just make sure you don't get too close." He spread his arms wide and gave them a broad smile.

"Welcome to Mars, legionnaires."

18.

The day after landing, the legionnaires were given a couple of hours off, except for a small force on standby. Ethan's squad was among the lucky ones, so they set out in pairs and small groups, along with most of the rest of the cohort, to explore Camp Elysium. The base had a surprising number of shops and places to eat and drink, each with their separate airlocks. Ethan had been expecting some kind of dome covering the base, but Optio Sharon, who'd spent several tours of duty here, explained that domes might be practical, but vulnerable. Mars wasn't the most exposed place when it came to Lumin attacks, but if one did come, a single blow to a dome structure could prove catastrophic. Ethan nodded, it made sense. Ethan walked with Optio Sharon at first, and when the old soldier disappeared into one of the watering holes to meet some old acquaintance, Helena, Gavin and Erwin Rauch joined him instead.

He saw her immediately once the four of them entered a small taco place to get some lunch. He stepped out of the airlock, and stood watching her for a moment. The way her neck craned sometimes, the black hair with a shade of red when the lighting was just right, the shape of her back when she sat, just a little straighter than the ones next to her.

"I'll go grab a table," Gavin said. Ethan nodded. He didn't even notice when Helena and Erwin followed Gavin to the table. He took a step forward, and stopped. He didn't know what to say. It had been so long since they had seen each other. Since she promised to wait for him. And then there was Eileen. He felt guilty, eager, and confused, all at the same time. He walked again, and stopped. Some of the ones sitting with her looked at him, and she turned to see.

"Optio Ishmael," he said, way too formally. She smiled, blushing a little.

"Decurion Wang." She got up and came to meet him. They embraced. She kissed him on the neck.

"Ethan, it's so good to see you. Finally."

"The same," he murmured. "Malika, I don't know what to say."

"Don't say anything. Come, let's talk. There are a few more private stalls in the back." He followed her and they found a vacant stall, with walls separating them from the other guests. As soon as they sat down, she began speaking.

47

"It's been so long. Ethan, I waited for you, I really did..." She trailed off. Ethan sensed there was a "but" coming, but he had some confessing to do before he let her spill her guts.

"Malika, I slept with Eileen." There it was. She didn't reply, so he kept going. "We were stationed at Ceres together, and... Well, I... I'm sorry, it wasn't planned or anything."

"I did it too, Ethan. I'm so sorry. I did a tour in the asteroid belt as well, just a few months ago. So many in my unit died. When we returned here, well, it was as if being alive made it okay. It wasn't, and I've been kicking myself ever since."

"Eileen died," Ethan said. He didn't know what else to say. Malika lowered her eyes.

"I know. I ran into Antonio on my way here. I'm sorry, Ethan. I truly am."

"Yeah, me too. Not because, you know, but she was one of us." Malika nodded. They both knew that when you'd gone through basic together there was an invisible bond between them, one that would remain no matter what happened later.

"I think I have to get back to the others, they must be wondering," Ethan said.

"Ethan," Malika said, taking his hand. "What's going to happen? I mean, I guess we're not... Are we still friends?" Ethan noticed her eyes - those big, brown, beautiful eyes - were turning moist. He cleared his throat.

"Yeah, Malika. We're still friends. Perhaps, in time..." She nodded.

"Perhaps, in time," she repeated, forcing a smile.
Ethan turned and walked back to the others.

19.

The starship from the Blue Sector Confederacy (BSC) was too different from anything built by humans to describe. Of course, BSC technology was widely used by human starships, but it wasn't as if the BSC shared everything they had. For instance, human starships were orbit bound, relying on transports of various kinds to ferry people and materiel to and from the surface. The BSC starship, on the other hand, easily penetrated the atmosphere, traversing the sky like a meteorite, until it finally came close enough to land, invisible forces aerobraking until the ship stood nearly still in mid-air. It slowly descended until it stood quietly on the platform, surrounded by legionnaires lined up tightly to welcome the envoy.

Ethan stood in front of his squad, who had a clear view as the alien envoy exited the ship, after a huge glass-like dome rose up to cover both the ship, the aliens and the welcoming committee led by the commander of Camp Elysium. BSC bodyguards, vaguely human-looking, but taller and wider, and wearing matte black, unfamiliar armor and helmets with silver visors covering their faces, stood to either side inside the dome, weapons ready.

Standing just outside the dome, with a clear view of the arrivals, Ethan couldn't stop staring at the BSC envoy. It looked like a thin stick of wood that moved, with two spidery limbs on either side, in addition to the two "legs". Its skin and clothing both looked like bark and only when it moved did he see that it was indeed wearing some sort of fabric. Behind the envoy, a knot of aides followed, most of them from species Ethan had never even heard of. One looked like a swirling cloud of dust, changing density from one second to the other. Another looked like a mix between an otter and a hippopotamus, only with leathery bat-like wings that moved along with its "arms". The weirdest one was probably the floating blob of water, or that was how Ethan would have described it.

Then there was the human. A beautiful brunette of about forty, in a slick outfit that looked like a uniform but not quite like anything Ethan had ever seen, gracefully following right behind the representative itself. He was surprised, since he didn't know the BSC employed humans. Then again, what did he really know about the Blue Sector Confederacy?

As soon as everyone inside the dome left for the reception and talks, the legionnaires not assigned to guard duty were dismissed. Second platoon was to be deployed on the side of the dome closest to the perimeter fence, and Adjunct Levinson issued his orders to the squad leaders. He pulled up a display which had three red rings on it, marked one, two and three.

"First squad you're up by the northern edge here. You'll have three behemoths supporting you if anything should happen. Second squad, take the middle point. Make sure at least two of your HMGs are placed near this hill. If anything should happen this is the likeliest point of entry. A set of behemoths should be there already. Third squad," he said and looked straight at Ethan. "You will man the southeast corner. Cohort didn't have any behemoths to spare, but this is the least likely point of entry for an attacker, since they would have to move through this dense minefield, exposing themselves well before reaching the fence. Nevertheless, I want you to spread out and cover the area just in case."

"Yes sir," Ethan replied. The adjunct dismissed them, and Ethan led his squad out. First he put Optio Sharon's fire team in place, where the experienced soldier had a good view of the minefield. His own team was placed in the middle so he had a good direct comms view with each of the other teams. Optio Warren's fire team manned the southernmost part of the area, where a fossa, one of the many deep trenches covering the landscape, made up a natural barrier that protected the area.

"All right, you all know what to do. Heavy weapons placement first, then I want you to dig in ASAP. I don't care about likelihood of attack and such. Dig as if you were expecting an imminent attack. Execute." Everyone did as they were told, and he noticed Optio Sharon giving him a small nod, and a smile.

Ethan got to work with his own fire team, and soon they were digging defensive positions as if they were actually going to war.

51

20.

Ethan didn't know how long the alien envoy planned to stay, or when they were going to be replaced, so he made a simple rotation order for his squad. He and Helena would take first watch on his team, manning the HMG, while Gavin and Erwin rested, leaving the rocket launcher position ready to spring to life, should anything happen.

"So Dec," Helena began as they were both watching the minefield through their optics, "I'm sorry it didn't work out with Malika." Ethan eyed her sideways.

"What do you know about that?" he demanded.

"Just what everyone else knows. You two were a thing, and that ended yesterday."

Ethan turned back to observing the naked landscape.

"Well, I guess it ended a while ago, really," he murmured.

"You mean, when you slept with Eileen Green?" she pressed on. He turned toward her again, sharply.

"What the hell, does everyone know everything about me?"

Helena laughed softly, smiling.

"No no, but this is the Legion. Rumors spread fast." Ethan let out a heavy breath.

"You're right, of course. Anyway, I guess we both realized we're too young to be a couple. None of us were ready for it." He paused for a moment.

"Wait a minute, why am I talking about this with you? I'm your squad leader goddammit. Let's just... Let's just drop it right now, okay?"

Helena nodded, still with a smile on her face, and they both went back to observing the landscape.

About ten minutes later it happened.

A loud bang, followed by small arms fire shattered the silence.

"Alarm, unknown attackers are coming up from the fossa," he heard Optio Warren's voice through the helmet comms. He called it in on the common channel. Gavin and Erwin had already joined him and Helena.

"This is one two three, we're under attack. Enemies coming from the southern fossa," He switched to the squad channel. "Third squad on me, we're engaging in force. Sharon, get your butts over here."

Less than a minute later Optio Sharon's team came running.

"No word from Warren?" he asked. Ethan shook his head.

"We'll have to assume they've been overrun. Everyone, this is for real."

The eight legionnaires moved out and slowly walked toward Optio Warren's position. When they were about fifty meters away from where the team had been placed, Ethan saw a legionnaire lying on the ground, with a big hole in his back. Obviously there was nothing they could do, so they kept moving.

The attack came mere seconds later.

"Incoming," someone screamed. A rocket missed them by a hair and exploded behind them.

"Get down, but maintain line of sight," Ethan shouted. He didn't have to shout, as everything he said could be clearly heard through the helmet comms, but it was a habit that everyone seemed to stick to in combat situations. He got to his knees, and took aim, looking for something to fire at. A burst from Optio Sharon's HMG told him the enemy was coming.

Then he saw them. Human height and build, black suits, helmets with gold visors. He fired, as did the rest of them, and several enemies fell. The black clad enemies kept coming, pouring forth as if they had all the manpower in the world. Ethan was certain the enemy had lost at least twenty soldiers, but it was as if they didn't care.

He looked around. So far no legionnaires were down, except the ones from Optio Warren's team. But there had to be more than fifty of them now, some hidden behind low rises and others firing from the knee or prone positions. It seemed they only had light weaponry, interspersed with a few rocket launchers, so the legionnaires' HMGs and rockets gave them quite a match.

A claxon began blaring in the distance, and Ethan saw what had to be a gunship flying toward them from the west. If they could just hold on for a few more minutes...

A scream through the comms interrupted his thoughts. He immediately saw that Erwin, the new guy, was down.

"Gavin, what's Erwin's status?" he asked. Gavin just shook his head, took aim and fired another rocket.

Then he hunkered down as low as he could, and did the reloading himself.

The gunship swept down behind them, and did a low flyover. Every legionnaire hugged the ground as the gunship's machine cannon began to chatter. Ethan risked a quick peek and saw enemies running away, toward the fossa, only to be cut down one by one. He stayed down for a few more seconds, until the gunship had passed, before he slowly got up. The silence was eerie. He walked forward, and other legionnaires followed. Dead enemies lay strewn everywhere. He heard a commotion from behind, and saw that more legionnaires were approaching, probably from first and second squad, who were the closest.

When they came to where Optio Warren and her team had been, they found the dead bodies of the three remaining legionnaires, including the optio.

Ethan walked over to one of the enemy casualties, and turned him over. Then he sat down, and clicked the gold cover so that only the glass visor remained. The sight of the dead soldier within surprised him, although some small piece of him had probably expected it. The enemy was human.

21.

Ethan was summoned later that afternoon, after a thorough debriefing session. Adjunct Levinson and Centurion Farrow walked him to the reception area, where they were able to remove their helmets. The human aide to the BSC envoy met them.

"I'm sorry Centurion, Adjunct, only Decurion Wang from here on," she said, in the softest velvety voice Ethan could imagine, and displaying a perfect smile of impeccable teeth. It was almost as if everything about her was too perfect, which made Ethan nervous.

"Decurion, would you please follow me? Envoy Rizzikit is waiting for you" she said, and turned without waiting for an answer. Ethan took a double step and hurried after her. He noticed that she had a shapely butt, but before he could take that thought further, she stopped in front of a set of double doors. Flanking the doors were two legionnaires, one a decurion and the other a senior decurion. For a moment Ethan wondered why they would use NCOs as guards, but then he realized these were spec ops, handpicked personnel, usually with years of experience. Who else would serve as bodyguards for the alien envoy? Of course, it was only natural that most of them would have gained rank throughout their service.

The decurion knocked the door twice, and it opened from the inside. As soon as he and the aide stepped through he noticed the alien bodyguards standing off to the sides. Their human-like posture, offset by their enormous size, was vaguely unsettling. Then he looked ahead, and saw the BSC envoy itself, sitting in a lounge chair in the far end of the room. It was wearing a re-breather mask or something, but otherwise looked quite comfortable. It beckoned with one of its "hands".

"Come, come closer," a machine voice said. Envoy Rizzikit was using a translation device, and only when Ethan concentrated hard he was able to make out a few of the envoys own sounds, more like leaves rustling in the wind than an actual voice. He stopped in front of the envoy. Only the human aide remained, and Ethan assumed it was because of the atmosphere in here. The envoy needed a re-breather; other kinds of aliens may not be suited for this kind of atmosphere at all; the watery blob came to mind.

"Ethan Wang, you led the charge against my enemies, the ones trying to assassinate me, and I would like to thank you personally. You showed great courage, attacking an enemy that came too close for comfort. Tell me, did you see anything unusual?" Ethan told the envoy about the attackers being human, which it clearly seemed to know already.

"There are a number of humans," Envoy Rizzikit said, "scattered throughout several systems, who don't like the Blue Sector Confederacy. Oh sure, they liked it well enough when we saved you from the Lumin invasion, but afterward humanity has shown itself as a hard nut to crack. Even the Earth government, who have staunchly supported human membership in the BSC, sometimes make unreasonable demands, like Earth having its own currency, or your refusal to submit your soldiers to the common defensive league, insisting on fielding your own military. Well, suit yourselves, those are all demands the BSC has conceded. But the ones you met today want to isolate Earth, to withdraw from the BSC altogether. They say the government is corrupt, that the BSC is like a Trojan horse, that we will stab you in the back somehow. Nonsense, of course." The envoy pointed one of its stick fingers at the nearest bodyguard.

"Humans should realize they are an inferior race in many regards. In fact, you ought to look to the Khargiz, who are practically your cousins, genetically. The Khargiz are true servants of the BSC, having thrown in their lot with us several centuries ago. They are richly rewarded for their submission, and we even have a standing fleet posted in their system for protection. An invasion like Earth suffered would never happen to the Khargiz." It withdrew its hand and leaned forward.

"But you, Decurion Wang, are a prime example of the better properties your species are capable of. By reacting like you did, you did the Blue Sector Confederacy a great service, and you should be richly rewarded. So I have an offer for you, a great honor indeed." What could only be interpreted as a smile spread across the envoy's face.

"Would you like to become part of my personal bodyguard?"

22.

"Squad, on me. Quietly," Ethan whispered into his helmet comms. The night was cold - nothing compared to Titan, of course, but enough to feel it even through the suit's insulation - and it would be tempting to hurry along. Especially on routine duty like this.

"Nothing much happening, Dec," Gavin whispered back as the first scouts began filtering in. Soon they were gathered in a semi-circle around Ethan, with just a single guard off by herself, watching the scanners and sensors they had set up to cover the area. Optio Sharon was the last one to come in, and he gave Ethan a small nod as he took a knee.

"Right, we'll move on in a few minutes. Let me just check in with Siobhan first, and then I'll report in." Ethan called up Siobhan Rutherford, one of the legionnaires assigned to his team after they lost five to the assassin attack. She was the one in charge of the scans and sensors, and seemed more than competent. Ethan wondered why she wasn't in training to become a tech.

"It's quiet, Dec. Only heat signatures around are the prison guards, and if we weren't already closer than we ought to be, we wouldn't pick up on them either."

"Good. Legionnaire, I want you to stay on point, and pick a course through those dunes. I want us to be back inside the perimeter before dawn."

"Will do, Decurion."

Ethan addressed the others.

"Siobhan's picking a course back for us. Hold back for a few minutes, before we move out."

Everyone got back on their feet, checked their weapons and made ready to move. Optio Sharon came on to the one-on-one private channel.

"Dec, I just can't figure you out," he said, chuckling. "Here you are, saving the BSC envoy's ass, then he offers you this posh job. And you refuse him! No, not just that. Even after he explains what an insult it would be to decline, you still refuse. What..." Ethan cut him off, one of the nice things about outranking him. It

59

even worked that way with the comms as well, and Ethan suspected, no he was sure, it was made this way on purpose.

"Optio, that's enough. It was my choice and it would be again." Then he added, "by the way, who are you to speak? You should be an officer by now, on merit and experience alone. Who are you to speak about insulting the wrong people?"

"Sir, that's different. The sticks, they see things differently. Man, you really offended him..." Ethan cut the line, waited for a moment, and thought back to his meeting with the envoy. To be honest he didn't consider how it would react when he refused. He just didn't like the creature, or its attitude. That was all. And he'd be damned if he was to serve as bodyguard for someone like that.

He opened the squad channel.

"Siobhan, how are we doing on time?" he asked. Dawn was less than three standard hours away.

"Dec, we should be fine. About an hour if we move quickly. Double that if we take our time."

"Fine. We'll take our time, no matter how quiet it is. I don't want us to be surprised again."

23.

Camp Elysium was big enough that a decurion might have been given a private room, so it was by design that Ethan had to sleep on a bunk in the same room as the rest of his squad. Something to do with team spirit or squad cohesion, he guessed. Right now though, it was impractical. He was going to speak to some of his squad members individually, in private, and instead of doing so in his room, he'd have to go find a quiet place to speak. He settled on a corner in the platoon's common room. Most of the platoon were on duty so he hoped it would be reasonably quiet.

The first to enter was Siobhan.

"So, you've been with the Legion for almost a year," Ethan began while pretending to read her file. He'd already read the files of everyone in his squad, and knew most of it by heart. It was an icebreaker though.

"Yes, Decurion. After Basic, I was sent here and that's basically it." Ethan nodded.

"Have you thought of getting specialty training? I see you're good with the scans and such. I think you'd be good Tech material." Siobhan smiled and Ethan realized he might have been too blunt. He was supposed to beat around the bush for a while, apparently. Not his style though.

"Straight to the point, Dec. I'll be straight as well. Yes, I have thought about it. My high school grades would prevent it though. I really slacked off in school, and if I hadn't done pretty well on the test at the recruitment center I doubt I'd be here today. But I've heard grades count for specialization."

"Maybe so. To be honest, I have no idea. But what if it didn't?" he asked.

"Then yes, I suppose I'd like to try out for Tech."

"Good, I'm sending applications today. I just need your signature."

She scribbled her signature on the form, and that was that.

The next one was Gavin.

Ethan already knew Gavin's preference, having spent time with him since their trip to Ceres.

"So, you think the Legion can make a heavy trooper out of you?" Ethan asked, grinning. A heavy trooper himself, he knew what it took, and he believed Gavin was the perfect candidate.

"That's for the Legion to decide. I'd like them to consider me though."

"Well, let's not waste any time then." Gavin signed the form, leaving Ethan with one legionnaire left to speak to.

The three he'd chosen were those he considered to have the best potential for specialization, but in the days to come he might speak to a few others too. Jared Poole on Optio Sharon's team might make a decent medic, having volunteer experience before his enlistment, and Kyra Stephens, one of the replacements, had let it slip that she might want to apply for Cavalry training.

Helena was the last one today though, and he smiled and offered to grab some coffee as she sat down.

"So, Helena, I guess you know what we're here for," he said, and she nodded.

"The thing is, you're one of my most capable legionnaires, and I think you're an obvious candidate for specialization. Only, I don't know anything about which one."

"I was thinking about medic..." she began, but trailed off as Ethan shook his head.

"I'm sure you'd make a great medic, Helena. But I've seen you in combat. I want you manning some kind of weapon. You're smart, so you could make it in Tech as well."

"I don't think I'm strong enough for Heavy Infantry..."

"You sure about that? You've manned the HMG often enough, with me. And if you get exoskeleton certified that's more like Tech than Infantry, to be honest.

"Or perhaps Cavalry," she said.

"Mhmm, sure. You're tall though. Just below the max limit for Cavalry."

They sat for a moment.

"Decurion, I have a question, nothing to do with this," she said eventually. Ethan motioned for her to speak.

"The prisoners. I know we're not supposed to speak of them, but... I spoke to someone who told me there are political prisoners there as well, not just violent ones. Sir, I mean Dec, why would they put political prisoners here? On Mars, I mean?" Ethan didn't know what to say, so Helena kept going.

"Do you think they've been sent here in order to avoid fair trials?"

"Now, I wouldn't assume..." Ethan said, but he still didn't have a reply. Political prisoners. He'd heard there were people opposing the unified government of Earth, or its membership in the Blue Sector

Confederacy, but he'd never met one. Or rather, he'd never met one until the assassination attempt on the BSC envoy. And those were definitely the violent kind. Why would anyone oppose any of it? It didn't make any sense.

Then he remembered Dan Carruthers and Robbie Alsop, who had bullied and tormented and almost killed Jed back in Basic. They would be serving sentences somewhere on Mars. He told her about it, and even how Jed had committed suicide after the accident.

"Now, that's the kind of people they keep here. I really wouldn't be too concerned about their welfare if I were you," he said.

Helena nodded slowly, and didn't speak of it again.

"So, about this form..." Ethan said, indicating the specialization application form.

"Well..." she began, "it would have to be Heavy Infantry or Tech."

"Legionnaire Neuwijnkel, listen. I just got Siobhan's signature, she's applying for Tech. You know she's good at that stuff. Now, you also know Tech is a small specialty, and they will only take so many. So I want you to add two and two together, and when you do, the conclusion should be obvious. If I were you, I'd apply for Heavy Infantry. I'll give you my warmest recommendations, promise."

Helena nodded to herself for a moment. Then she reached out and grabbed the form. She signed at the bottom, and smiled.

"Decurion, I think I'll make a good heavy trooper." Ethan smiled back at her.

"I'm sure you will. And let me say, I hope to have you back on my squad one day."

She hesitated for a moment, and it was as if she wanted to add something. Then she nodded, once.

"Me too, Dec. Me too."

24.

Ethan swore as he checked his weapon for the umpteenth time, using the special brush to dust off red sand, which immediately began building up again. The weapons should be able to handle anything, even the sandstorm which had plagued this part of the planet for the last six months, but he didn't trust it one hundred percent. He still longed for days of clear skies and visibility beyond what was straight in front of him.

The squad had a lot of rookies, and only he and Optio Sharon remained of the original crew. Gavin and Helena had left for Heavy Infantry training some four months ago, and two months ago Siobhan had been accepted to Tech training. In his spare time Ethan now found himself spending most of his time alone or with the other decurions of the platoon, Ben Snow and Lisa Carr. Sometimes he'd talk to Optio Sharon, but the veteran legionnaire was more of an advisor than any ordinary friend.

He knew Julian was still around but the Tech people were usually kept on the far side of Camp Elysium and seldom mingled with the others. Most of

65

what they were doing was probably top secret anyway. Only Ariel would sometimes bump into him. She headed one of Decurion Snow's fire teams, and as far as Ethan could tell she was well on her way to a promotion. He, on the other hand, seemed to have reached a dead end. It would be years until he made Senior Decurion, which would normally be the most experienced NCO in the platoon or even Century, and he wasn't even twenty yet.

Ethan was tired of the routine, tired of endless patrols through empty plains and treacherous fossae, constantly battered by the sandstorm that seemed to go on forever, obscuring what would otherwise be a beautiful landscape. He wondered, not for the first time, if he'd been right in refusing the BSC envoy's offer. He could be traveling the galaxy now, seeing new planets and alien races, instead of slogging along, covered in dust. The only interesting parts were where the red dirt was broken by the occasional patch of lichen, one of the few visible proofs of the terraforming projects that would last for hundreds or maybe thousands of years. What if he'd taken the offer, would he be happier? Then he remembered the stick, which was the term the legionnaires had adopted amongst themselves for the envoy's species, and the first thing that came to mind was its derogatory attitude toward humans. He remembered how he'd felt at the thought of serving this creature. The stick was gone now, of course, with the entire entourage, off to some other subject race, to remind them of their place in the universe and of who called the shots.

In a way, Ethan realized he understood why some people would oppose the BSC's dominance, although he still didn't think any of that justified assassination attempts or active resistance against the Earth government. Granted, Earth had become a subject of the BSC, and there was a definite order of things, where aliens such as the stick stood way above humans, but on the other hand, Earth had been allowed a fair degree of autonomy, even to the point of having its own military forces. From what he'd learned, that wasn't always the case among the BSC worlds.

He sometimes wondered what the political prisoners Helena had mentioned had done, whether they had advocated violence or simply voiced their opinions at the wrong place and wrong time. At the thought of the prisoners, he realized his squad should be right next to the prison's outer border. It was just a line on the map, so there was nothing indicating where it ran. He had to check their position to know whether they were approaching it or not.

"Squad, halt. Let's take a two minute break," he said into the helmet comms. He put two legionnaires on guard, while the rest of the squad hunkered down, trying to find some cover against the wind, enough to brush off their weapons, if nothing else. Optio Sharon and the other team leader, Rowe, came over.

"The nav unit seems off," Optio Sharon said. "I counted the fossae, and we've already crossed five. There are only four of them outside the prison perimeter. Either we've crossed one of them twice, meaning we're moving in circles, or the nav unit is leading us further east than we ought to be."

"I didn't notice," the other optio said. Ethan hadn't expected him to. Optio Rowe was fresh out of Heavy infantry training, and didn't have any combat experience yet, whereas Sharon had years. He kicked himself for not thinking of the same thing. He'd been too absorbed by his thoughts.

"This sandstorm is messing with the nav for sure, it's not the first time," Ethan said. "But if we are inside the perimeter, we'd better get the hell out of here before the guards notice. They don't like legionnaires sticking our noses into their business."

"Should we backtrack?" Sharon asked. Ethan thought for a moment before answering.

"No. We know the perimeter is most likely west of us. We'll move forward and move northeast. That way we won't have to cover the same area twice."

"Want me to take point with my team?" Optio Sharon asked. Ethan nodded. He could always count on the grizzled veteran.

"Do it." Then he switched to the squad channel.

"Squad, move out."

25.

"Dec, something's going on here." Optio Sharon said on the comms. Ethan signaled with his hand for the remainder of the squad to stop. Others relayed the message to those further away.

"Talk to me," Ethan said.

"We're definitely inside prison territory. A work gang just passed us. Some twenty prisoners and two guards. But here's the strange part, only one guard was armed, and the other, along with a few of the prisoners, looked hurt. One of the prisoners even had an emergency kit covering his torso. Looks like his suit was ruined, and the emergency kit's what's keeping him alive, at least for now. The rest of them looked okay, but they seem to be moving as fast as they can. You may be able to intercept, or you could move west and avoid them altogether. Your call Dec."

Ethan thought about it. They weren't supposed to be here, but on the other hand, people were hurt, and something had done that to them. Their mission was basically to sweep the area east of Camp Elysium without entering prison territory, but now that they had crossed the border already, shouldn't they figure out what was going on? He made a decision.

"We'll intercept and figure out what the hell is going on," he said. "Optio, bring your team back here, quickly but quietly. We don't know what's happened to them, and if we're headed toward a fight, I want the squad intact before we engage."

"Will do, Dec," Sharon replied.

Ethan made sure everyone was informed, before moving on. Two of the legionnaires used scanners to locate the work gang, and found them within minutes. Optio Sharon and his team reunited with the rest of the squad before Ethan gave the order to establish contact. The squad moved forward, carefully, weapons ready.

When they hailed the armed guard, the reaction was different than expected. Everyone knew the prison guards didn't like legionnaires, and that right now Ethan's legionnaires were walking on forbidden ground. So when the guard lowered his weapon and came forward, and began almost hugging the nearest legionnaire - as much as anyone wearing a closed system suit with a helmet could actually hug - Ethan's eyes widened. The legionnaire was taken by surprise too, and pushed the guard away.

Ethan switched to an open channel designed to communicate with anyone nearby.

"What the hell has happened to you guys?" he asked.

The guard tried to recompose himself, but it was one of the prisoners who answered.

"Decurion," she said, surprising Ethan by knowing the Legion rank system. Not many civilians knew of the Legion, and fewer still knew their ranks. "Thank you for being here. I have no idea what you're doing inside the perimeter, but thank God you're here. They are going to slaughter every guard and prisoner alike before they move on to Camp Elysium. That is, if they're not moving on Camp Elysium already"

"What are you talking about? Who?"

"The Lumins. The ones we ran into didn't follow us because they seemed to be moving straight west, toward Camp Elysium." Her voice faltered for a moment, before she repeated, "Decurion, the Lumins are here, and they are coming in force."

26.

Ethan questioned the prisoner for a few minutes before he called it in. He learned that the prisoner's name was Joan Teller, and she claimed to be have been a political activist back on Earth. She mentioned getting arrested after organizing a rally against the imprisonment of a well-known scientist, but by then Ethan had to cut her off. They didn't have much time, so he managed to get as much detail on the Lumins as possible. That was the main thing right now.

"Did you see them yourselves?" the officer he was relayed to asked sourly. "We have absolutely no indication of an impending attack."

"Sir, with all due respect, that's why they call it a surprise attack. We did not see the Lumins ourselves, but we've seen what they did to the guards and prisoners. One of the prisoners just died by the way, from his wounds."

"Well, that's not good enough. We need confirmation, not some prisoner's tale."

"What about the guards? They say the same thing," Ethan tried.

"As I said, we have no indication..."

"Sir," Ethan shouted into the mic. "Let me speak to Tribune Jeremiah Tanner. He knows me and will speak to me."

A few minutes passed, before Ethan heard a familiar voice.

"Ethan, what's going on?"

"Sir, they are here. The Lumins are here, and they are coming for Camp Elysium. Some dumbass desk jockey doesn't believe me, but I'm telling you, they are coming."

"You sure about that?"

"Yes sir. They are moving in from the east, using the sandstorm as cover."

"Alright, I believe you Ethan. Thank you," the tribune ended the conversation.

Ethan had the squad establish a defensive perimeter. He didn't know if they would be able to return to camp the same way they'd come, but he sure knew they wouldn't be able to contribute anything by joining this fight. This was a battle of bombs and cannons and rockets, not a small patrol of infantry.

Soon they heard attack ships overhead, and soon explosions could be heard in the distance. The sound of fighting got more intense, and Ethan figured the area between them and Camp Elysium would be crawling with enemies.

"Miss Teller, would you expect the Lumins to attack the prison before or after Camp Elysium?" he asked.

"I don't know... My guess is they would rely on surprise to take on the main force, so I'd think the prison would be attacked by a smaller force, after they initiated the fight at Camp Elysium."

Ethan nodded to himself. That had been his thought as well.

An idea began to form in his mind.

27.

"Decurion, your squad is to sit this one out. You did a good job warning us of the attack, now leave us to it." The officer said. Ethan didn't know her name, only her rank. Centurion. He'd been relayed straight to her after identifying himself, so he guessed he'd spooked the first one he'd reported to properly.

"But ma'am, I think we might be of use defending the prison. It's not far, and the guards will need any help they can get." The officer surprised him when she chuckled.

"The guards are not there to defend the prisoners. Look, Decurion, if the prison is overrun, their orders are to dispose of every prisoner there. It's no big loss, just murderers and traitors, the kind you don't want to risk the necks of your squad for."

"What'll happen to the guards?" Ethan said, mostly to hide his disgust with the officer's answer.

"They will find a way to escape. If not, they will die knowing they served the interests of humanity with honor."

Ethan ended the conversation and sighed. He thought about what the officer had said. The prisoners would be "disposed of" she had said. Did that mean the guards would willingly murder every prisoner there? From what he'd seen of the interaction between the prisoners and the two guards that were here, that would be unlikely to happen, but he couldn't be sure.

He walked over to where Joan sat with a few others, and pulled her aside.

"I'll be blunt," he said. "What would happen if the guards were told to kill all the prisoners?"

"I take it that's not something you just happened to think of," she said slowly, frowning. He didn't reply.

"Okay, either the prison has some sort of kill switch, like releasing gas into the cells or something. If not, there would be a fight."

"You think the prisoners would be able to fight back?"

"No. It would be guard against guard. You see, some of them are okay. Others would execute any order, no matter how immoral." Ethan thought for a moment, before he shook his head.

"I don't think it would come to that. The higher-ups wouldn't risk it. And I'm sure they know there are bound to be amicable relations between some of the guards and prisoners. Especially in an outpost as isolated as this."

"So, a kill switch then."

"Most likely. Once the order is given, one guard, an especially reliable one, from their point of view, would push a button, and every single prisoner would be dead within minutes.

28.

"Well, you know I'm in," Optio Sharon said. Ethan was glad to hear the veteran agreed with him. He turned to Rowe.

"I'll follow any order you give me," the optio said. Ethan nodded knowingly. Optio Rowe wanted assurances that Ethan would take the full blame for what they were about to do. He intended to.

"Good, then gather the troops. We're moving out in five minutes. Each team; leave one legionnaire to guard the civilians. We'll rally here afterward.

Ethan went to tell the prisoners what to do, while the optios got the legionnaires ready. Everyone was already combat ready so it didn't take long. It took longer to convince the prisoners to stay put.

"Look, we cannot have prisoners coming back there, the guards would freak out. We cannot arm you anyhow, so you'd be of no use. Besides, we are trained soldiers, a cohesive unit, and we'll fight like one. You'd only be in our way." Ethan wanted there to be no doubt.

"We're bringing one guard only, to make sure the others understand the gravity of the situation. That's it." He left without waiting for another argument, another reason he should bring some of the prisoners along.

Soon after, the squad which now consisted of a mere nine legionnaires, moved east toward the prison. All the while the sounds of battle could be heard through the thin Martian atmosphere, and flashes would occasionally penetrate the sand that otherwise covered their view of what was going on in the skies above.

Twenty minutes later they reached the barbed wire fence that separated the inner prison territory from the outside. Two of the legionnaires quickly cut their way through, and soon everyone was standing in front of the prison wall itself. The guard stepped forward, identifying himself through the comms. Then he contacted his superior.

"Sir, I'm relaying you to Decurion Wang of the Ghost Legion, the guard said as Ethan was patched into the conversation."

"Decurion, this is Captain Lavans. We have specific orders, and these do not include taking orders from... Legionnaires."

"Sir, I do not ask you to take orders. I ask you to reconsider the situation. With our help, you might be able to avoid fighting the Lumins, which would surely void your... Final order. I'm sure you understand, I am not trying to have you break a direct order. I'm merely trying to change the situation so that order isn't necessarily your only option."

"A fine way of putting it," the captain replied. "Nevertheless, what would nine legionnaires change? You would be outnumbered, surely. Which leaves us with the final order."

"Sir, I have fought the Lumins before. I think we can outsmart them. Let me ask you, do you and your men want to live?"

29.

Ethan watched as the prisoners were marched out, chained to a long wire and watched by armed guards. The legionnaires stood to either side, eyes glued to scanners that would warn them of any impending attack by the Lumins. Ethan took one final look at the prison as Captain Lavans closed the gate.

"This better work," the captain grumbled as he walked past him. Ethan forced a smile, meant to assure him, but the captain had already passed. Then he walked over and checked the charges. He flipped a security switch on his remote and made sure the light turned green. Then he flipped the switch back, and put it in his pocket.

He walked back to where Optio Sharon stood waiting for him.

"Get them to the rally point as quickly as you can. Then move everyone south, as far and as fast as you can. I'll catch up. You're in command now, but if you get in any trouble this was my plan, my orders. Got it?"

The optio nodded solemnly, or at least that's how it looked through the visor. Then he saluted Ethan, who saluted back.

"Get moving, Optio," Ethan said. Sharon turned on his heel and moved away, along with the rest of them. When they were out of sight, which wasn't far in this weather, Ethan lay down to wait. He couldn't see the prison from here because of the sand covering his view, but his scanners worked just fine, and would detect any heat or moving objects in the area. He sighed. He was too close for comfort, but he needed to make sure the connection held. He looked at the remote. Still green.

The Lumins came from the North, as he'd expected. At first they spread out in a half-circle before they began approaching the prison. Ethan didn't dare take a look, so he waited. Only when one of the Lumins screeched something, which to Ethan sounded like it discovered the trap, did he press the button.

The explosions came less than a second apart. Six charges, spread across the outer wall, two that took down the guard tower and quarters and four that reduced the cell area to rubble. And if he was lucky, the Lumins would be right in the middle of it all.

He risked a quick peek, but the visibility was zero. He crawled closer, and soon he was able to see the outer wall. Or rather, he saw where the outer wall had been. Now it was nothing left, except a few carcasses of mech droids, blown apart. No sign of Lumins at all. One of the carcasses moved slightly, before it lay still.

Ethan crawled back. When he felt sure he was out of reach of most types of scanners, he got to his feet. He brushed off the red dust, before he began moving south.

30.

Ethan caught up with the others by nightfall. Optio Rowe laughed and Sharon patted him on the back. Captain Lavans congratulated him on saving so many lives, but warned him this wasn't over until the prisoners were delivered back to Camp Elysium. They kept moving south, to make sure they got away from any pursuit by the Lumins, but this time they got lucky; no Lumins appeared.

When Ethan got back in touch with camp Elysium, his transmission was immediately scrambled and routed to Tribune Tanner, who congratulated him on discovering the threat before the Lumins could launch a surprise attack that might have succeeded. Because of his early warning the attack on Camp Elysium had been averted, and detachments of legionnaires were now mopping up the final stragglers. A starship that had been previously cloaked was spotted leaving Mars orbit, and Tribune Tanner told Ethan he suspected it was headed for Titan, which was still held by the enemy.

"About the prisoners..." Ethan began.

"Don't worry about it Ethan, it's outside of Legion jurisdiction," Tanner said.

"Sir, I know but..." Then Ethan told the tribune what he'd done, and how they were now on their way back with the prisoners, some of whom needed medical care.

"You just couldn't stay away, could you?" Tribune Tanner sighed.

The next day Ethan walked through the southern gate into camp Elysium, heading a column of legionnaires, prison guards and prisoners. Legionnaires from other units stood to either side of the column as they passed by, and Ethan noticed more than a few nods and smiles.

A detachment of regular troops took charge of the prisoners, and Captain Lavans gave Ethan a final nod before hurrying along with the rest of the prison guards. Joan Teller was nowhere to be seen, but Ethan had a strange feeling he hadn't seen the last of this strong-willed woman.

"Decurion Wang," a voice behind him commanded. He turned around. A lieutenant from the regulars stood beside a Tribune he didn't recognize. Behind them stood a small team of four regular troopers.

"Please come willingly," the lieutenant said. The Tribune, an olive skinned man with a scar across his left eye, snorted loudly.

"Or we can drag you along kicking and screaming, I don't care." Ethan wondered where Tribune Tanner could be, he would have sorted this out. He gave his weapon to one of the regulars, figuring he had no choice.

"I'll come," he said. Then he followed the officers away, with the troopers surrounding him. Optio Sharon seemed about to attack them singlehandedly, but Optio Rowe and a few of the other legionnaires held back the hot-tempered Israeli.

He was led to the entrance of an underground facility, away from the Legion barracks, guarded by regular troopers. They quickly passed through the air lock, and entered a long hall with what appeared to be cells on either side. He removed his helmet, and one of the troopers took it from him. The lieutenant motioned for him to enter one of the cells, holding the door open for him. He looked inside. The room held a single mattress and a bucket serving as a toilet. The smell of urine and shit was almost unbearable.

"Sir, what the hell is this?" he said.

Someone shoved him brutally inside. When he turned the troopers stood aside and the tribune came to stand in the doorway. They scowled at each other for a moment, before the tribune spoke.

"Decurion, you really have no idea, do you? Those prisoners? Did you know that four of them were among the top echelon of the resistance back on Earth?" Ethan shook his head, but the tribune didn't seem to notice. "If our hands weren't tied behind our backs, they'd be executed a long time ago, but unfortunately they are serving life sentences instead. Then, by pure providence, we have a shot at getting rid of them, a convenient defensive measure, surely, who can fault anyone for that? But wait; here comes Decurion Wang and his rogue legionnaires, disobeying a direct order, saving the four worst enemies of society in one big sweep. Wonderful, just wonderful."

Then he slammed the door shut with a loud bang that echoed through the hallways.

31.

Ethan was started awake by the shouts and noise from outside. He didn't remember falling asleep on the dirty mattress, and now that he noticed he stood up. The old soldier instinct, to sleep whenever he could because no one knew when the next chance might come, had probably kicked in at some point during the night. He felt sure it was night, but with no light and no clock available, he could be wrong. The shouting drew his attention, and he tried to listen, to hear what was being said.

Before he could make out any coherent words, the door burst open, and Optio Sharon stepped inside.

"Son of a..." He began. Then he saw Ethan and stopped.

"Decurion, are you okay?" he asked. Ethan nodded, and followed him through the door. The optio sneered at the bucket as he walked out - luckily, Ethan hadn't had to use it yet - and turned toward the lieutenant, who stood at something near attention, with an eye that looked like it was swelling shut fast. A legionnaire held a gun to the officer, while another held one to one of the guards. The other guard was down and being given first aid by another legionnaire. As the one giving first aid turned toward him, he realized it was Malika. Then he looked at the other legionnaires and recognized Julian, Ariel, Decurion Snow, and four new ones from his squad. The Tribune who had arrested him was being held in a corner by Decurion Carr and Optio Rowe, and another figure stood in the shadow, away from the others. The figure stepped forward, and Ethan recognized Tribune Tanner.

"Well Ethan, we're making some powerful enemies today," he said, with a grin that Ethan found discomforting. "On the other hand, it was bound to happen some day anyhow, so why not do it on our terms?"

"Sir, all of you... You shouldn't have put your necks on the line for me..." Ethan swallowed. Tribune Tanner shook his head.

"Of course they should. *Legio Patria Nostra*, those are not just words. It means something for all of us. We're not letting a fine soldier sit here and rot because of some scheming political bullshit. But just to be clear, we're all acting on orders here. The Legate signed the order an hour ago. Sure, he needed some convincing, but I can be very persuasive. Besides, how would it look if regulars could arrest any legionnaire they didn't like? No, we take care of our own, and serve justice on our own, if need be. In your case, I don't think that would even be an issue. But either way, it's a question of jurisdiction."

"Bloody traitors!" the Tribune in the corner screamed.

"Tribune Espinoza here doesn't seem to agree with his superior," Tanner spat and turned toward the captured tribune.

"You do realize the Legate - the Legate himself, no less - the commander of the Ghost Legion, is your superior as well. Even though you've been licking the boots of regular brass for years, you're still a legionnaire. Formally, at the very least."

"You've all gone crazy," Tribune Espinoza said. Tribune Tanner laughed.

"True, I've been known to cultivate that image," he said. Ethan smiled, remembering the weird test administrator an eternity ago.

32.

After locking up Tribune Espinoza, and the regular lieutenant and guards, the legionnaires locked the building from the outside and took off. They didn't move towards the Legion barracks, as Ethan might have expected, but instead set a brisk pace toward the spaceport. A dropship stood waiting for them, and as soon as they were all on board the craft lifted off. Ethan removed his helmet, and took a deep breath.

"What's happening, Tribune? Where are we going?" he said. Tribune Tanner held up a hand and removed his own helmet.

"Right now we're set to rendezvous with a starship in Mars orbit, that's all I can say for now. Once we get there we can speak more."

As soon as the forces of acceleration let off, Ethan unbuckled and floated over to the single porthole, where Julian sat. They both looked outside.

"If we switch places you can see more of what's in front of us," Julian said. "In fact, you should." Ethan wondered what he meant, but they switched places, and Ethan laid his face up against the porthole in order to have the best possible view forward. Then he realized what it was.

A small armada of starships appeared, still far away but moving closer fast.

"How many are there?" he whispered.

"I counted eleven big ones, and who knows how many dropships, transports and fighters," Julian replied. "A few of the big ones are dreadnoughts, battleships, but most are troop transports. I guess you could fit the entire Legion into those ships."

"I knew you were a clever one," Tribune Tanner said, chuckling as he took a seat beside them. Then he pointed at one of the ships, barely visible still. "That one right there is the Excelsior, which I assume you're familiar with, Decurion. Well, right now it's the home of First cohort, and in five minutes we'll dock onto her." He paused and chuckled again. "Remember that I said the Legate signed our orders to set you free, Ethan?"

Ethan nodded. "Yes sir."

"Well, we weren't in his office when he did. We were standing outside the transport that would ferry most of Legion command up to its new headquarters, in space." He waved toward the armada. "That there, is almost the entire Ghost Legion, and we're the final stragglers." Ethan was at a loss for words, but Julian seemed to catch on.

"This is big," he said, "this is really big."

"It sure is," Tribune Tanner replied.

Part 3

33.

As soon as they docked with the Excelsior, Ethan and the others went through the airlock. Gravity kicked in as soon as they passed through the inner hatch where they were met by an adjunct he hadn't seen before.

"Are we the last?" Tribune tanner asked. The adjunct nodded.

"Yes, sir. There's going to be a briefing in one hour. I will take you to your quarters. Follow me." The adjunct began walking.

"Well, this is where I leave you," Tribune Tanner said as they crossed an intersection. "Good luck everyone," he said, and walked away.

"Good, there you are," a female voice said, and Ethan turned to see it was Tribune Falck, commander of First Cohort. "I take it none of you are informed of your units yet." No one answered, as it wasn't really a question.

"So, First Cohort has been designated as heavy infantry. We'll receive more heavy troopers from Second and Third, along with a fresh batch out of Camp Piteaa, while our lighties will be assigned to cohorts appropriate to their qualifications." The light troopers from Ethan's squad were led on by the adjunct, while Ethan, Ariel, Optios Sharon and Rowe stayed with the tribune. The Tribune continued. "Optio Ishmael will be serving with First Cohort Staff as medic, and Optio Brooke, you will serve on First Cohort Staff as well, in the Tech Unit. You two can come with me. Decurion

Carr, Decurion Snow, you will have squads of your own. Optios Rowe, Chambers and Sharon, you will be serving in Decurion Wang's heavy infantry squad." Ben Snow and Lisa Carr walked off to find their own units, which would have rooms nearby as they all belonged to the same century.

Ethan and the others entered a large squad-sized room, and Tribune Falck walked away, along with Malika and Julian.

"So, should I salute you now?" Ariel said, grinning. Ethan smiled back at her.

"You know we don't do that," he said, before he hugged her tightly. It felt good having friends like that, and he knew he'd have to break it off before he got too emotional.

"Finally! I've been dying to serve in a heavy unit again," Optio Sharon exclaimed. "Of course, it was a pleasure serving in your unit back on Mars, Decurion..." When Ethan just laughed, the optio continued. "But I'm a heavy trooper first and foremost, as are you, I believe."

"We've never actually served in a heavy unit, just trained for it," Ariel said, "but I'm looking forward to it."

"I wonder where we're going," Optio Rowe said.

"Not many places left if they want us to fight Lumins. In this system, at least," Ethan said, and knew he was right. "As far as I know, only Titan remains. We've chased them off from everything else. It only makes sense to clear Titan before we go anywhere else."

"Yeah, I think you're right," Ariel said. "Besides, they're sending the entire Legion. They really mean it this time." That last comment was clearly meant for Ethan, who had been there the last time the Legion sent forces to Titan, only to be slaughtered by the Lumin mech droids. Out of two full cohorts, only five legionnaires had survived. Ethan wanted revenge, but the thought of going back sent chills down his spine.

34.

"Greetings legionnaires," Tribune Falck began. The commander of First Cohort had appeared a few seconds before on large screens in every common area of the starship. Ethan had taken his squad to an area shared with the rest of First Century, and many familiar faces stood beside him, watching and listening as their commander spoke.

"Last year our Legion suffered one of its greatest losses ever, when two entire cohorts were annihilated by the Lumins on Titan. It was, to be frank, an ill-prepared and ill- conceived mission, and those responsible have received their just punishment." Ethan, not for the first time, wondered who was responsible, but both cohort commanders were dead, and the only one higher up that he knew of was the Legate himself, who he'd never seen or heard. He figured it had to be someone in staff or intelligence positions, and the only one he knew of in such a position was Jeremy Tanner, who apparently hadn't been punished. He assumed it was because Tribune Tanner had nothing to do with the Titan disaster. Anyway, it was all brass business, way above his head.

"Now the time has come, to take Titan back from the Lumins. After cleansing the asteroid belt and the remainder of the solar system of their poison, Titan remains their last outpost. It is well defended, but with the might of the entire Ghost Legion along with several Earth Defense battleships, and with intelligence gathered by the Titan survivors and later probes, we shall defeat them. The Ghost Legion spent a year licking our wounds and replacing our losses, and now we are stronger than ever." Ethan looked around. He had been green himself the last time, as had so many others. Now that he saw fresh legionnaires, just out of basic training or specialization, he wondered, had he looked so naive? So convinced of his own immortality? He returned his gaze to the screen.

"The attack on Mars was their final straw, an attempt at gaining a foothold when all others failed them. That didn't succeed, and now they have strengthened their defenses on Titan instead. If we manage to chase them off they will have no bases within lightyears' distance from Earth. Which is the way we prefer it, obviously."

She paused and the program skipped slightly.

"First Cohort, you are to spearhead the assault." A few murmurs broke out among the legionnaires. It's a recording, Ethan realized, tailored to each cohort. Smart move, this way she could address everyone separately, at the same time. The message became much more relevant than just the usual honor and pride talk that the brass was so fond of.

"Shut up and listen everyone, this is us," Centurion Farrow barked. The legionnaires quieted and concentrated on the screen.

"As a heavy cohort you will be inserted a few hours after the bombing begins, to establish a beachhead near the Lumins' main base. Your ground assault will begin immediately when air to ground operations cease, and your mission is to force a path for Second and Third Cohorts, which will land once the beachhead is secured. Similar operations will take place elsewhere on Titan, with heavy infantry paving the way. A century from Tenth cohort, which is our new all Cavalry cohort, will support your attack. Now, since we expect heavy resistance, including Lumin air units, a fighter wing from the regular forces has been assigned to support your assault. Because of the delicate political situation at the moment, I will ask you to be careful trusting the flyboys. The Legion is currently balancing on a knife's edge, and there are elements among the regular forces leadership who'd rather see a defeated legion replaced by regulars, even if it means leaving Titan to the Lumins for now. Hopefully the air wing will be true allies in this fight, but just in case of a betrayal, I have seen too it that every platoon has extra surface to air capacity. Just in case."

So, Ethan thought to himself as he exchanged glances with a few of the others, we may have to fight our own as well as the Lumins.

"Well, if this isn't turning into a real field day, I don't know," Ariel muttered. Ethan didn't answer.

35.

Ethan gathered his squad after the briefing. Optio Sharon and Optio Rowe stood there, of course, as did Ariel. These were his fire team leaders. Then there were Helena Neuwijnkel and Gavin Samson, who came straight from heavy infantry training at Camp Piteaa. Both wore fresh bold square markers that signified their new qualifications. Both were also beaming, obviously happy to be serving with a familiar squad leader. Ethan grinned at them and shook their hands.

"Good to see you both," he said. "And congrats."

The remaining six legionnaires were a mix of second and third cohort. Ella Holston was the most experienced of them, having served for three years in the Legion. Trevor Green came close with two years in the regular forces before he joined the Legion. Zia Carver wasn't as experienced, but Ethan immediately noticed her competent manner, and she had an impressive dossier. He wondered why she hadn't been bumped to optio yet. Rico Shaw was the only South American, and though he seemed like a good soldier his previous CO had noted that he tended to let his emotions get the better of him sometimes. Ethan quickly decided not to hold it against him. He sometimes tended to do so himself. Lars Johnson was a Swedish-American, who had experienced the Lumin invasion first hand as his parents escaped the carnage with him and his younger brother. No lack of motivation there. The last member of the squad was Roger Flint, a Californian who had finished a degree in engineering before joining the Legion. Ethan wondered why he hadn't been picked for tech duty or something more advanced. He made a note to find out some day.

"Okay then. I think we'll make a good squad, no a great squad. But we all need to learn to operate together. Some of you already know each other, but we have different roles now. So, the sooner we start training as a unit, the better. And believe me, if any of us are to survive Titan, the more training, the better. Titan is an unforgiving place. Believe me, I've been there."

36.

The next day, after hours of practice in the Century's training facilities, someone called out his name.

"Decurion Wang, I was hoping to find you here," a man in his mid-twenties said and strode toward him. There was something vaguely familiar about him, but Ethan couldn't put his finger on what it was. He recognized the silver sparrow on his lapel though, and stood at attention.

"Adjunct, I don't think we've met," he said. The adjunct smiled and seemed to hesitate for a moment.

"No, I don't think we have. At ease, Decurion." He paused for a moment. "I am honored to meet you, and to serve in the same Century as the survivor of Titan." The he extended his hand.

"Adjunct Stephen Miles. I believe you served with my brother, for a short while."

It dawned upon Ethan then, that this was the younger brother of Centurion Miles, who died shortly after landing on Titan. It seemed like a thousand years ago, and at the same time he could remember every detail as vividly as if it was yesterday.

"Adjunct Miles, yes, I knew your brother. So sorry about your loss..." Ethan hesitated, trying to remember if he'd seen the adjunct before. "It's strange, I haven't seen you around. I do attend at least some of the officer meetings, whenever they allow us NCOs to take part," he said.

"Well, I never go there," Adjunct Miles said. "I may be an adjunct, but as far as officers go, I'm probably not what you'd think of as an officer at all. I mean, rank-wise, sure, but I don't command anyone." He smiled.

"I'm a tech specialist, actually you may call it a specialist among specialists. Not to brag, of course..." Ethan noticed the adjunct blushing. No, he could see that this was a guy who preferred to work alone. So different from his brother. He liked this guy already.

"I have a friend, from back home actually, who's a tech. Perhaps you've met him, Optio Brooke. I know he's on the Excelsior."

"Oh, yes, I know Julian. In fact, he's training with me, although I doubt he'll go all into systems as I have. No," Adjunct Miles looked up at the ceiling, musing, "I'm a true geek, while I think Optio Brooke is more of an all-round techie, the kind who gets attached to combat units. Or maybe a combat tech unit. You know, he's the one who told me that you were here."

"Well, Adjunct Miles, it was a pleasure getting to know you, but I have a lot to do right now, so if you'd excuse me..."

93

"Of course, of course. Like I said, I'm honored to serve with you, Decurion."

Afterward Ethan walked over to a lounge chair and sat down to watch some news that was running on a big wall screen. So far he'd heard nothing about the fighting on Mars, only a number of stories of the victorious Earth Forces kicking the Lumins out of the Asteroid Belt. No mention of the Mars prisoners or the surprise attack that had been averted. No mention of Titan. Most civilians had heard that the Legion had suffered a blow on Titan a year ago, but that was never mentioned anymore, and Ethan suspected most civilians didn't even know that Titan was a moon, not a planet.

In fact, Ethan was beginning to suspect the public was only told what served the purpose of the governing elite. It was an outrageous thought, but after meeting a genuine dissident, and finding her quite likable, he had begun to wonder what his role as a legionnaire was. Was he a soldier fighting for the liberation of what should by rights be human territory, or was he, in fact, a puppet serving other less honorable purposes?

"Hey Levi!" he shouted, to get Optio Sharon's attention. The Israeli came over, raising his eyebrows slightly.

"Dec," he said, waiting. Ethan chewed his thumb for a moment before speaking.

"You've been a soldier longer than most, longer than anyone I know. Except some of the brass perhaps." He said. Levi Sharon nodded.

94

"Tell me, how do you do it? How do you go on? I mean, have you ever wondered if you're doing the right thing?" The Optio shook his head.

"Never, Dec. The Lumins came to take what's not theirs. We have every right to take it back."

"Of course, I'm not thinking about the Lumins... But the dissidents, what if... Ah, I don't know..."

"Decurion Wang, if I may give you a sound bit of advice, you only need to worry about two things. First the big picture, and I mean the really big picture. Us or the Lumins. The survival or the extinction of the human race. Then it's the really small picture, like your squad, your platoon, your century. You know, your fellow legionnaires. Everything in between is a distraction, a false track, one you don't want to go down. Do you understand what I'm talking about Dec?" Ethan nodded. He knew the veteran was right. He shouldn't worry about politics or rivalry. None of that mattered when it came down to it. He stood up and turned his back on the screen.

"You're right. It's probably the waiting." Sharon nodded gravely. As a veteran soldier, he should know everything there was to know about waiting.

37.

Ethan was escorted by a senior decurion through the corridors leading from the elevator to the Legate's chambers. Legate Camus was legendary, although Ethan had never seen him, other than a few pictures, taken in his younger days. Legate Camus had become well

95

known as one of the heroes of the Lumin War. As the commanding officer of an elite Special Forces unit, he had been one of the leaders of the Unification, which brought Earth's former governments to heel. Ethan tried to remember what he'd read and heard about Legate Camus, or General Camus, as he was known back then. A great general who had fought the Lumins since the beginning, then one of the leaders of the Unification, and then... Nothing. At some point during the Consolidation he had vanished from the public eye. Ethan didn't doubt that the general had kept on fighting, but he had left the political scene, only to reappear as the commander and one of the founders of the Ghost Legion several years later.

The senior decurion stopped outside a door guarded by two legionnaires.

"Decurion Wang, here to see the legate," he said. One of the legionnaires checked a wrist pad, and nodded. The other pressed his hand to a plate beside the door, and the door slid to the side. The senior decurion walked in and Ethan followed.

Inside, they stopped and stood at attention. Before them stood a white haired man with a strong jaw and ice blue eyes, uniformed and decked in medals and honorifics.

"Thank you Senior Decurion. Now, please leave us. I would like to speak to Decurion Wang alone." The senior decurion immediately complied, and closed the door behind him when he left.

"Decurion Wang. First, let me congratulate you on a job well done back on Mars. Although you did stir up a bit of trouble... Heh!" The legate laughed, before he walked over to a lounge area and sat down.

"Come, sit with me, please," he said. Ethan followed and took a seat, trying not to get too comfortable. After all, he was in the presence of a legend.

"So, I've been told you met with Joan Teller," the legate said, startling Ethan.

"Sir, I didn't know at the time... But yes sir."

"Don't excuse yourself. Never."

"I spoke to her, Legate." When the legate motioned for him to continue, Ethan blurted, "She struck me as a knowledgeable and wise woman, not at all like a crazy rebel."

"Ha ha," the legate laughed, "she tends to have that effect on people. Did you know she was one of us back when you were just an infant? She was a powerful leader back then. The Unification was at least partly her plan." Legate Camus leaned back and stared at a point far, far away. "It was the demands of the Blue Sector Confederacy that pushed her away. She said she couldn't stomach the thought of humanity being ruled by an alien race, dictated by representatives sent from some world hundreds of light years away." A question Ethan had thought about on several occasions came back to him, and he figured he wouldn't get a better chance to ask than right now.

"Sir, pardon me, but wouldn't you say dictated is a strong word? The BSC doesn't seem all that interested, to be frank." The legate looked at Ethan, and smiled.

"Son, what do you know of the rules laid upon Earth by the BSC?" When Ethan didn't answer Legate Camus laughed.

"Don't worry, not many get to know the inner workings of the BSC and their presence on Earth, including the rules humanity must abide by." He shifted and leaned toward Ethan.

"No spaceflight beyond the asteroid belt, unless officially sanctioned by a BSC representative. That's right, we're not even allowed to defend or explore large parts of our own system."

"Then what about Titan, Sir?"

"Titan? Well, the last one was sanctioned. This one is not." Ethan was taken aback. They were violating the rules set by the BSC. What kind of punishment were they risking by doing that?

"Ethan, here's another one. Whenever a BSC representative commands it, Earth is to deliver a force to fight on the BSC's behalf, wherever they wish. That's one of the reasons the legions were created; they are faster to muster, and can operate relatively independent of other forces."

"Sir, is this common? Has the Legion been sent on such missions before?" The legate nodded.

"Several times, and a few of them have cost us dearly. We lost an entire cohort, including a starship, on Oxtaba, seven years ago."

"Oxtaba, sir?" Ethan replied. He remembered hearing the name before, although he had no idea what kind of place it was.

"Oxtaba was a worthless hell hole on the far side of the galaxy. I have no idea why they wanted us to do their dirty work for them there, and I don't want to know. The less we speak of it, the better." He paused.

"So you see, Decurion, there are degrees when it comes to standing up to the BSC. I am not an insurgent, and yet, I do rebel from time to time against the dictates of the Blue Sector Confederacy. As does the Earth Government from time to time, in their own way. But we try to stay within certain limits. Joan, well, she went too far. And now she is an outcast, a pariah." He shook his head. "It's a shame."

Legate Camus rose slowly, grimacing from what could only be an old injury as he stood. Ethan followed suit.

"Well, Decurion Wang, it was nice to finally have a chance to chat. I'm sure we'll speak again soon." Ethan saluted his commander, before he turned on his heel and walked out the door.

38.

The starship had entered a stable orbit several hours ago, and now it was circling the moon where Ethan had barely survived almost a year ago. Titan was down there, though the surface remained hidden, covered in a thick layer of clouds. Ethan turned away from the viewing screens. Some might find the view beautiful, but he didn't. To him, Titan meant death. He caught the eye of Ariel, who also didn't seem all that interested in watching. He forced a smile.

"You ready for this?" he said. Ariel, quieter than usual just gave him a quick nod.

"Once we get down there I'll be all business," she said. "It's the waiting that does it for me." He gave her heavily padded shoulder a squeeze.

"We'll show them this time," he murmured.

Helena and Gavin were standing by, waiting for his orders. The squad was back to four three-man fire teams again for this particular assault, and Helena and Gavin were on his team.

"Why can't we just board the dropships already?" Gavin asked. "I'm sure there are more than just me who would like to have some extra time getting into my exo." They would be wearing exoskeletons this time around, powered armor fitted with all kinds of heavy weaponry. The exoskeletons were mounted securely inside each dropship, and instead of putting them on, as they would with ordinary armor, they would enter the exos as if getting into a special seat. Only when the ship touched the ground would the exos be released.

"Your exo will be ready, and we'll have plenty of time. Look, the bombing will take hours. Better to wait here. Get some shuteye if you can. Who knows how long it'll be before you get another chance? Or watch the show if you can't sleep."

Optio Sharon was going through some details with his fire team, and nodded to Ethan as he walked past. Ethan nodded back. Of all the troopers in his squad, no, in his platoon, Sharon was the one he respected the most. The grizzled veteran always knew what to do.

Ethan lay down on his bunk, and closed his eyes. He wondered how he'd react once he returned, once he landed on this godforsaken moon. So many had died. The Lumin mech droids had slaughtered them wholesale. But this time would be different. Surely, it would be different.

"Whoa!" he heard someone shout, followed by excited chatter.

So this is it, he thought. The bombing of Titan had begun. He rolled over, but sleep wouldn't come.

39.

Ethan got back up once he realized he wouldn't be able to sleep. He walked out to where some of the others sat around, watching the live feeds that showed the bombing from above. Orbital bombing had to be one of the most effective ways of ruining a world completely, he thought, while pictures of impacts filled the screen. So far, there had been no attempt to counter-attack, and Ethan assumed the Lumins had gone underground while the four battleships attached to the Legion rained death from above.

"The recon drones are on their way down," Adjunct Levinson said. "They should be sending live images from the ground in just a few minutes." Ethan nodded and took a seat next to Optio Sharon.

"Looks like New Year's Eve from up here," the Israeli said drily. "I don't think the Lumins see it that way though."

"Since when did you care how the Lumins see things?" Ethan replied. Sharon snorted.

"Ha, I don't. I'm just saying, looks can be deceiving. It all depends on your point of view."

Ethan sat quietly, waiting for the feed from the recon drones to begin. Sure enough, a few minutes later a blurry image appeared and sharpened a bit, before it swept across the wrecked landscape. For the first minute or two it seemed like they had bombed empty stretches of ice and slush, but then smoking ruins appeared, and a cheer rose from the legionnaires.

"That'll show them!" someone shouted.

A wrecked mech droid appeared, and the drone zoomed in on it. It was cut in half and one leg was missing. The drone zoomed out again, and moved on, into the ruins. A body that looked almost human appeared, and Ethan stopped breathing for a moment, realizing it was a Lumin. It lay face up, frozen stiff, with its helmet visor open. There were no apparent injuries, but in the temperatures on Titan, injuries often didn't show because everything would freeze over. Ethan wondered what had happened to it; had it been hit and opened the visor without thinking, or had it opened the visor and died from that? The drone swept by continuing deeper into the ruins.

Suddenly a burst of flame appeared to its right, and the drone shook. It turned as if to flee its attacker.

As they watched, the legionnaires heard a loud rattle as from a machine gun, and then the image went blank.

"Well, that was it guys," Adjunct Levinson said. "Now we know for sure there are still live enemies down there, even after we've bombed the shit out of them. Not that we expected anything else." Ethan nodded. The bombing had taken its toll on the Lumin defenses, but as always the ground forces had to do the dirty work. Titan was still in enemy hands, and it would be up to the legionnaires to take it from them.

Centurion Farrow entered the doorway, and stood facing them.

"Listen up. It's boarding time. Make sure you're tightly secured inside your exoskeletons, remember to check your air supply. We land fully armed, magazines in weapons, safety on. As soon as we hit the dirt, I want rounds chambered, safety off. Got it? Then move out."

40.

The dropship hit the ground hard, and Ethan felt as if his insides were tossed around. It took him a moment to realize the light on the exit hatch was still red. He moved his left arm and chambered a round in his 12.7 Cal HIPR, Heavy Infantry Personal Rifle. He flipped a switch, safety off, and carefully kept the weapon aimed in the safest direction possible, toward the hatch. Then he pulled a lever on his shoulder mounted rocket launcher, arming it, but keeping the safety on for now.

"We're down, aren't we?" someone said. Ethan looked toward Adjunct Levinson, who looked like he was having a conversation inside his helmet. Something wasn't right.

"What's up with the hatch?" That was Ariel, speaking to him.

"Stuck, apparently. Don't know why."

Something struck the side of the dropship, and it felt like it slid sideways.

"Listen up!" Adjunct Levinson said. "We took several hits on the way down, just before landing, and the pilot is dead. We're sitting ducks here, so we need to get out fast. However, we've landed on a slope, and right now the tilt is increasing, so there's a risk the craft may start rolling."

Ethan unstrapped himself and took an unsteady step forward.

"Allow me, sir," he said, and without waiting for an answer he fired his HIPR, carefully avoiding the reinforced area in the middle of the hatch. The heavy rounds punched through and exploded inside the heavy hatch, weakening it, and short-circuiting any electronic controls holding it in place.

"What the hell!" someone shouted as a fragment zinged by.

"Hey, you're armored, remember? Now, move away, back here," Ethan shouted and hit a button on his virtual control panel. Something whirred inside his rocket launcher, switching from the previously armed missile to a smaller, more versatile rocket. As soon as he got a green light, he fired.

"Crazy son of a bitch!" someone said.

The hatch exploded and flew outward. Ethan moved forward through the smoke.

"Third squad, follow me!" he shouted, moving as fast as the exoskeleton legs would allow in the cramped compartment. Outside he saw the dropship was indeed tilting, dangerously so. As the rest of the platoon swarmed out, the tilt increased steadily.

Just as the final stragglers were exiting, it began rolling. Ethan caught a glimpse of Adjunct Levinson's characteristic red helmet marker before the wrecked dropship started barrel-rolling down the slope.

"We've got company," Decurion Roberts from first squad shouted. Ethan turned and saw a small group of mech droids approaching. He felt the hairs on his back rising, remembering the last time he'd seen these deadly war machines at work. Ethan took charge without thinking.

"Concentrate fire on the mech droids, each squad work together, take them out one by one. First squad start on the left, third squad start on the right." An explosion behind him made him turn. The dropship, with Adjunct Levinson and a few legionnaires still on board, went up in a ball of flames.

Ethan wondered what had hit it, but then he realized he had enough to worry about.

Every surviving member of the platoon was firing at the mech droids, and soon the enemies were reduced to rubble.

"Whoa, this feels better than the last time, Ethan!" Ariel shouted. Decurion Roberts spoke on the common channel.

"Platoon, we've lost Adjunct Levinson."

Ethan swept at his virtual screen until he got the entire platoon's life vitals up before him. True enough, the adjunct and three others had gone from green to red.

"Decurion Trellis is wounded as well, got his leg chewed up," Roberts continued. "Decurion Wang, you have been here before, you should be in command now." Ethan coughed.

"Decurion Roberts, both of you are my seniors," he said.

Optio Sharon spoke up, "Ethan, listen to me. Decurion Roberts is a smart legionnaire. He knows that your experience here is more valuable right now than a few more years in the Legion. Listen to him, and lead on."

"Everyone," Decurion Roberts spoke without giving Ethan a chance to protest, "Decurion Wang is in command of the platoon until we receive new orders from Century." he turned toward Ethan, waiting.

"Ah great..." Ethan grumbled. Then he gave his orders. "Decurion Trellis, pick a legionnaire and stay back until Century medics can come and get you patched up. Senior optio of second squad, that'll be Rollins, right? Take charge and reorganize the fire teams. First squad, move up to that ridge ahead, and set up fire teams, ASAP. Optio Sharon, I'm putting you in charge of third squad. Get ready to move out as soon as first squad is ready." Nobody protested, and everyone seemed to know what to do. Not too bad for a fresh platoon leader, he thought. Not too bad at all.

41.

"Decurion Wang, I'm sorry to hear of the loss of Adjunct Levinson," Centurion Farrow's voice broke here and there due to static, but Ethan got the gist of it. The platoon had moved quickly and they were now covering a stretch of ground just three kilometers away from the research facility that Ethan and the other survivors had broken into last year.

"I'm bumping you to senior decurion; battlefield promotion." The centurion continued.

"Thank you sir..."

"I'll spread the word. You're doing a fine job with the platoon. Now, here's what I want you to do. As soon as the cavalry comes, I want you to link up with them. The entire century will advance alongside the cavalry and hopefully we'll get air support in time as well. We're first in, it seems. Prepare the legionnaires. Out."

Ethan turned to his squad leaders, and gave them a quick overview of the situation. The he pulled Optio Sharon off to the side.

"Optio, do you remember Tribune Falck's briefing? Especially that last part about the fighter wing?" The optio nodded slowly, eyes narrowing.

"Do you expect trouble?" he asked. Ethan hesitated for a moment, but then he thought back on his unpleasant encounter with the regular forces back on Mars.

"I don't know what to expect. That's why I want half the legionnaires in third squad to be armed with anti-aircraft missiles. If something goes wrong, I want our reaction to be immediate and overwhelming. If it doesn't, fine, we'll just switch quietly back to regular missiles again."

"Got it, Sir."

Half an hour later a column of behemoths appeared.

"Here comes the cavalry," someone said.

Ethan was glad to see them, and when he saw the commander of the first vehicle standing in the top hatch he waved at her. The behemoth stopped, and he walked right up to it and looked up at her, noticing the black sparrow on her lapel. Seemed she had gained rank since the last time he'd seen her. She grinned as she recognized him.

"So, Ethan Wang, I heard you got your own squad now. Well done." Adjunct Morales, who had been his instructor during basic training, had never been a cheerful one. This had to be one of the first times he'd seen her smile.

"Well, thank you ma'am. Actually, I'm in charge of second platoon now, since Adjunct Levinson died only minutes after landing."

"That so. Alright then, are you ready to move out with us?"

"We sure are. Do we get air support?"

"Don't know. But the attack takes place in five minutes whether we do or not. Best get your platoon moving."

Ethan trotted off and informed the squad leaders. There wasn't anything else to do but wait, so they waited. Five minutes later the behemoths roared, and they began moving in on the Lumin stronghold.

42.

They were less than a thousand meters away from the stronghold when the enemy counter attacked. More mech droids than Ethan had ever seen came rushing out toward them, and for a moment he felt the cold of gripping him. Then his training and experience kicked in.

"Take cover!" he shouted. "First squad spread out to the left, second on me, third go right. Stick with your fire teams, and make sure you leave room for the cavalry to move."

Within seconds twelve fire teams were spread out and firing at the oncoming mech droid army. Behemoths rumbled as they passed in between the infantry, firing a variety of armor piercing rounds and high explosives as they moved. Ethan hoped the other platoons were as well prepared as his.

Then he received a priority message on his virtual control panel. He grinned.

"Legionnaires, we've got company. The air wing is here." Just seconds later, four fighters swept over them, firing their missiles into the enemy ranks.

Someone whooped, and Ethan ordered the infantry to advance alongside the cavalry. No Lumins, whether actual aliens or their droid servants, would stop them now.

As the first half of the air wing flew off and away from the battlefield, the second half appeared behind them. Ethan noticed they flew a bit lower than the first half, and he wondered why he hadn't got a new priority message. Then, as the first fighter released a set of rockets straight at the behemoths, he realized these weren't friendly at all.

"Third squad, get those anti-aircraft missiles in the air! The bastards are coming for us," he shouted. Immediately, Optio Sharon and half the squad turned and released their missiles at the fighters. Normally, infantry would have a hard time fighting off an aerial attack, but the legionnaires were well prepared, and several missiles hit home within seconds, before the enemy pilots could react. As two fighters exploded in mid-air, Ethan switched to the command channel.

"Adjunct Morales, how are you holding up?" he asked. A third fighter crashed into the ground, leaving just one that managed to get away, black smoke trailing behind it.

"Ethan, they got three of my behemoths and a fourth is limping. Looks like we'll have to abort the mission."

"Hell no, Ma'am! You've still got four fully functional vehicles, right?" Ethan blurted. They still had the momentum, and turning back now would let the Lumins repair and recover.

"I do, but..."

"Hold on a sec," he said, and switched channels again, without waiting for her reply.

"Centurion Farrow, this is Senior Decurion Wang. Seems you were right in your suspicions. The second half of the fighter wing attacked us."

"I just learned," the centurion replied. "And yet, most of your platoon's vitals look okay."

"They didn't attack the infantry sir. Instead they went for the behemoths. Took out four of them. Sir, I request that we continue the mission. We still have the initiative, and we'll make do with the four remaining behemoths."

"You sure about that, soldier?"

"I am, sir. If you could ask the flyboys, the first ones anyway, to do another sweep, I'd appreciate it, sir."

"Will do. Hell, they owe us big time now."

Moments later Ethan received a new priority message. The air wing, or rather, what was left of it, were on their way for another sweep. The planes couldn't have been grounded for more than a few minutes, to be back so quickly.

"Third squad remain alert," he said. "These should be friendlies, but I don't want any surprises. If you see anything indicating trouble, you fire everything you've got at them. Got it?"

"Got it, sir," Optio Sharon replied.

"First and second squads, move along with the cavalry. We'll break through this time. The rest of the century is hammering away at the aliens, and they can only take so much."

The fighters were back, and this time only the good guys. They let loose everything they had on the Lumins, and Ethan's platoon were the first to break through the enemy lines, passing wrecked droids and dead aliens as they moved into the Lumin stronghold.

43.

Ethan had expected fighting throughout the stronghold, down deep corridors and into heavily fortified underground facilities. Instead it seemed the enemy had broken once the Legion shot their defensive lines to pieces. Of course, the bombing had already taken its toll by then, wreaking havoc among the aliens. Everything around them was reduced to rubble, and even the buildings that still stood looked like a thousand year old ruins from another time. Four behemoths stood ready to charge at anything, while the infantry took cover behind them. Exoskeleton infantry were a mostly offensive weapon, able to charge at long distances, guns blazing, but idle waiting made them vulnerable.

"So, I guess we'll just have to go building to building now," Ariel said, as she stomped over to him on powered legs. "Shit, it's so torn up I can't tell one building from the next. Nothing looks like I remember it."

"There may be another option," Ethan mused.

"Listen up, everyone. We should try to make them surrender."

"How? We don't even speak their language." Ariel said. "We don't even know if they speak like we do; they may be telepaths or some shit, I don't know."

"Ethan is right," Adjunct Morales said, joining the conversation. Ethan looked up at her, sitting in the top hatch of her behemoth, wondering if she had any idea what he was planning.

"I want to start going building by building, but go easy on the explosives. I want a prisoner." He looked at the wrecked buildings again.

"Decurion Roberts, have your squad start over there," he said, pointing at one of the buildings. "Optio Sharon, you take the one next to it. I'm holding second squad in reserve for now. Go."

44.

"It will only speak to you," Optio Sharon said. "The first words that came out were "speak to Ethan Wang only", and that's about the only words I managed to get out of it. But hey, at least, it speaks!"

Ethan nodded, and checked his magazine. He had no idea why the alien only wanted to talk to him, or how the alien could know his name. He intended to find out though. "Let's go then," he said.

Optio Sharon had taken the Lumin prisoner in the third building the squad cleared, and he led Ethan over to the building where reinforcements stood watch outside. The two men stepped inside, and saw the alien immediately.

113

The Lumin looked like Ethan remembered, humanoid features although longer and thinner, high cheekbones, eyes that reminded Ethan of gems, like deep pools of indistinctive, shifting color. It sat strapped to a chair in the middle of a room that reminded Ethan more of a big living room than anything else. Around it, the squad, Ethan's squad from the Excelsior, stood holding their weapons ready. Some of them, like Rico, looked as if they would empty their magazine on the alien any minute. Everyone had their own reasons to see it dead, and Ethan took a moment to manage his own temper.

"Guys, give us some room," he said quietly. The legionnaires took a step back and a few lowered their weapons. He walked up and stood before the Lumin, not sure where to begin.

"You are being the creature Ethan Wang, ask?" the alien said. Ethan started. He didn't know what he had expected, but it sure wasn't the singsong voice, like an angel, that seemed to come from everywhere at once. He pulled himself together.

"I am Ethan Wang. How do you know my name?"

The alien smiled - it smiled!

"Ethan Wang, honored be I to meet, tell. Surrender to famous warrior most of all humans, do." The creature rose, causing a few of the strappings to pop open. So much for holding it captive, Ethan thought. A few weapons moved, but the legionnaires were disciplined enough not to pull triggers.

The Lumin bent to one knee, and held its hands out, palms up. Ethan noticed it had six fingers.

"Command, obey will I, tell," it said.

"Then tell me again, how do you know my name?"

The Lumin looked puzzled for a moment.

"Ethan Wang here, escape alive from big battle, living pictures of great warrior, tell. Observe Ethan Wang on small rock and red rock, is smart and difficult enemy, tell. Win battle again, know. Fear and wonder, Ethan Wang is reborn Rhoub the Arch Enemy of Lumin, ask."

"You have observed me?" the alien tossed its head to the side as it said "yes".

"And you think I'm the reborn Arch Enemy of your people?" Again the alien tossed its head to the side.

"Rhoub, tell," it said.

"Rhoub," Ethan repeated. "I don't know about that."

"What is your name?" he said.

"I Tsingatulare Dolibiotan Avaliea Tsetao Tsetoia Davaliatoan, female of the Wia Shoania Tealoare of Shototeoan, tell."

"I think I'll call you Tsinga, for now," Ethan replied.

45.

The interrogation was going slowly, but Ethan was learning more and more about the enemy. "You don't know our ranks, do you," Ethan asked. Tsinga tossed her head again in the affirmative motion he had noticed.

"What ranks is, ask?" she said.

"Ah, well... It's a way to tell who's in charge. Who decides."

"Understand I, do. Lumin have no need for ranks, tell. Know importances, significance, greatness, time not important is, tell."

"What do you mean by that?"

"Understand you not do, tell. Time linear Human way, know. Time not linear Lumin way, tell."

"You can tell the future?" Ethan asked.

"Is not like you think, tell. Future, past, not meaningful to Lumin, tell."

"Do you know who's going to win this war?" Ethan blurted. The alien smiled.

"Nobody know can, tell. Not how works this. It is... Possibilities infinite, we know all, tell."

Ethan was growing frustrated. He changed the subject.

"Why did you attack Earth?"

The Lumin looked like it didn't understand the question.

"I mean, why did the Lumin attack Earth?" That seemed to bring the message across.

"Understand now it you ask, tell," she said. "Lumin recognize Human strength, afraid of humans, tell. Many possibilities Human destroy Lumin, tell."

"So the Lumin were - are - afraid that humans may one day destroy them? Is that why?" Ethan said. Tsinga tossed her head again, without replying.

Ethan knew he was probably the only human being who had begun to grasp the Lumins motivations, and he probably knew more about them than anyone else alive. He needed to think, but he also needed to finish this.

"Alright, Tsinga, I want you to do something for me."

"Surrender to Ethan Wang, I, tell. Command anything, tell."

"Okay then. First, are there any spaceships left, or have we bombed everything you got?"

"Spaceships destroyed, many not all, tell. Underground deep, emergency ships ready, tell."

"Good. I want you to go, and take all Lumins that you find with you. Then I want you to make your way to these emergency spaceships, and leave. Leave this place, leave the solar system. Give your people a message from Ethan Wang of the Human Race: Leave us alone or we will destroy you."

"I obey, do, but..." Tsinga seemed to be hesitating. "If leave I do, I cannot serve Ethan Wang, tell. I am bound, tell." Ethan noticed her eyes darting from side to side, as if looking for a way out. He realized Tsinga's surrender was total; she would obey any command he gave. But knowing that this would be his final command seemed to upset her in a way that he hadn't realized. He put on his softest voice.

"Tsinga, listen. This is how you shall serve me. By delivering this message, you will do more for me than you could ever do in any other way. I will be eternally grateful. There is no way, no possibilities, future or past, that you may serve me better than by doing this. You understand this, I know you do. Since, well, all that about seeing time differently than us humans and all."

This time Tsinga tossed her head affirmatively, although slowly. Then she smiled, and spoke in that singing voice of hers,

"Understand I do, tell. Obey, I will, tell. For great purpose, thank I you, do." Ethan smiled as she stood up and ripped off the remaining restraints. She was at least two heads taller than him.

Ethan walked out in front of her, motioning for the legionnaires around them to back off. Then he turned toward the alien. Tsinga halted before him and looked him in the eye.

"Ethan Wang, thank you I, do," she said, before she bowed her head quickly. Then she darted off and disappeared out of sight. Ethan stood for a while, wondering if he had done the right thing. Then he realized he had done the only thing he could.

46.

"Senior Decurion, you let an enemy go. Just like that." Centurion Farrow was fuming, but he held it in check. If not for the color of his face, Ethan wouldn't have realized his commanding officer was furious at him.

"Yes sir, it seemed like the right thing to do," he said. "I told her to give her people a message; back off or we will destroy you. It seemed like a good idea at the time."

"It is "her" now?" the centurion said. "Seriously? And you think that message will scare them enough to back off, do you? That, instead of all the intel we might be able to extract from a docile prisoner, delivering a... a message, would be more helpful?" He had a point, and Ethan half- regretted sending Tsinga off. In the back of his mind though, he couldn't see how he could have done anything different.

"I'm sorry sir, I may have made a mistake..."

"You sure as hell did!" Centurion Farrow took a deep breath. "Nevertheless, you did lead the attack in an exemplary manner. Your platoon suffered no more casualties after you assumed command, you fought off the rogue fighter planes, and you took this place."

"Thank you sir."

Centurion Farrow fished up a small nondescript package from his pocket and tossed it over.

"Here, your new insignia," he said, and gave Ethan a wink. "I could have revoked it, you know."

"Thank you again, Sir," Ethan said. "Sir, I just came to think of something. What's happening to the fourth fighter pilot? You know, the one who attacked us?"

"We're holding him in custody. In fact, I don't know what will happen to him. But one thing is for sure, the Legion is going to be on its toes, now that it seems a faction of the regulars have attacked us."

Ethan kept thinking of his centurion's words as he walked out of his lander-turned-habitat. He was deep in thought when he turned a corner and suddenly stood face to face with Legate Camus. Four heavily armed bodyguards surrounded the legate and were about to make Ethan move aside when the legate interfered.

"Please, I would like to talk to this man," he said. The bodyguards took a step back, giving Ethan and Legate Camus some space.

"So, promoted once again, I see," the legate said. "Keep this up and you might take my job one day."

"Thank you sir, but I don't think I'm officer material. I don't even have a high school diploma." The legate waved his hand at the landscape surrounding them.

"Do you think a high school diploma, let alone a college degree, would be of any use here? No, there are other qualities needed in a place like this. Sure, my job requires a certain nose for politics, but other than that this is all pure soldiering."

"Well, in that case I might have you worried in a couple of years, sir," Ethan replied, and winked. That brought forth a grin from the legate.

"We'll see, Senior Decurion."

"Sir, speaking of politics... Our cavalry was attacked by four fighters, I'm sure you've heard. And I still don't get it, Sir. Why did it happen? Does it have anything to do with that situation back on Mars?"

The legate's face seemed to darken, and he nodded.

"Both Mars and this happened because there are opposing factions within Earth's government. I cannot tell you everything I know, but let me just put it this way; the Ghost Legion has left Mars, our main base off Earth for years, and we're not going back. We still have a few detachments on Earth, the Moon and elsewhere in the system, but maintaining them is getting riskier every month. In fact, we're in the process of setting up a new HQ right here, on Titan, which is about as far away from Earth as we can get. You can do the math yourself."

"So I guess getting a leave to return to Earth is out of the question, Sir?"

"Oh no, we're trying to maintain a facade of normalcy, so there will be leaves. We're just not putting all our eggs in one basket so close to any strong regular force that might become our enemy overnight."

"What about Mars, Sir?"

"Mars... No, we burned our bridges there. No legionnaires patrol the red planet anymore."

"For what it's worth Sir, I think that's a wise decision."

"I'm glad you think so, Ethan."

Legate Camus walked away and the bodyguards trailed after him. Ethan stood for a while, thinking of how different from what he had learned in school reality turned out to be. Unified Earth, a strong central government, Humans versus Lumins, and the Blue Sector Confederacy as the saviors of Earth in their hour of need. Nothing was quite like he had thought, and reality was far more complicated than he had learned. Far more dangerous as well.

47.

Ethan entered the inner hatch of the mobile habitat module, and removed his helmet. Most of his squad sat lounging in the common area, so he walked over to them.

"Hey," he said, "any news?" Ethan was waiting for a ride back to Earth, and rumors had it there might be room on the Excelsior, which was due to return to Earth orbit within a week for maintenance.

Instead, Optio Rowe nodded slowly, keeping his eyes down.

"Trevor got a message from home, his two sisters were killed in a terrorist attack, along with several others. His father barely survived."

"I'll go talk to him," Ethan said, removing his gloves. "Where is he?"

Rowe pointed at the doors behind the dining area, and Ethan walked over. He opened the door, saw that Legionnaire Green sat on his bunk, and entered.

"Trevor, I just heard..." he said, and sat down on the bunk opposite from the teary eyed legionnaire.

"My sisters were just six and nine," Trevor said. "They never hurt anyone. How can anybody..." He covered his face in his hands.

"I'm so sorry for your loss," Ethan said. He thought about asking what had happened, but he figured Trevor would tell him if he wanted to.

"It was a stupid parade," the crying legionnaire said. "Some kind of celebration of troops returning from the war. Mom had to go to work, so Dad took them to see the parade. And now..." He didn't finish. Then he looked up at Ethan.

"Senior Decurion, I have to ask you something; Is it true that you helped terrorists escape the Lumin attack on Mars?" he asked. Ethan started.

"No, is that what you've heard? No, no, first of all, those were political dissidents, for the most part. I don't think any of them were terrorists. And second, we brought them back to the base. As far as I know they're all locked up now."

"Yeah, I'm sorry. I just had to ask."

"Nothing to be sorry about. Look, I'll make sure you get on the first ride home, okay? I'll push on Centurion Farrow, and if that doesn't help, I'll go tell the legate himself. How does that sound?"

"Thanks."

Ethan stood up and gently patted Legionnaire Green's shoulder. Then he walked out again.

"Ethan, there you are," Ariel said when he entered the lounge area again. Ethan saw that Julian had come. He'd wondered what his friend was up to these days. Then he noticed the big D on his lapel.

"Julian, I see you're doing well. Not that I'm surprised." Julian grinned, and pointed at Ethan's insignia.

"Senior Decurion," he said.

"Yeah, well, it was a battlefield promotion. We lost our platoon leader, so I had to take over. Anyway, good to see you man. What have you been up to?"

"Well, some of it is classified, naturally, but I'm looking into droids mainly."

"Droids?"

"Yeah, mech droids, like those the Lumins have. I'm thinking we might be able to adapt them to our purpose and reprogram them. Lots of dead droids and parts around. We could build a small army of them."

"Nice." Ethan imagined what it would be like, having mech droids like the Lumins had, beside them instead of against them.

"So, you going back to Earth any time soon?" Julian asked.

"I have an open pass. Just need a ride."

"Sure you want to go back, with everything that's happening?" Ethan hesitated. Julian looked genuinely concerned. He put on a reassuring smile.

"Don't worry, it's not like civil war or something. Yes, there are factions that want to hurt us, and there are madmen and terrorists, but what's new about that?"

"Just be careful, will you?"

"Promise."

48.

It took six months until Ethan finally found a ride back to Earth.

He stepped off the bus at the nearest station and walked for half an hour until he stood outside the apartment building in the Spoke Corners District. He looked up at the worn building, a fond smile on his face. Then he unlocked the door and took the steps up. The sign on the door said Elsie and Ethan, and there was a clattering of kitchen utensils from within. He pressed the doorbell. Nothing. Need to fix this, he thought. Then he knocked.

"I'm coming, I'm coming," his mother's voice said. A moment later the lock clicked and the door opened.

"Hi Mom," Ethan said, smiling as the lump in his throat threatened to overwhelm him.

"Ethan," Elsie whispered at first, before she flung herself forward and embraced him. "Oh, Ethan, my boy!"

They hugged for a long time, before they walked inside. Ethan tossed his bag aside and gave her another big hug.

"Are you hungry?" Elsie said. Ethan shook his head. In fact, he wouldn't have minded a huge portion of Elsie's home cooked dinner, but he was dead tired. He felt like he could sleep for a year.

"How are you holding up, Mom?" he said once they stepped inside. "With the recent terrorist attacks and all?"

Elsie shook her head.

"I try not to think about it too much. Being afraid doesn't do any good. We've been busy at the hospital a few times though."

"Here too? In Atlanta?

She nodded.

"Nine attacks in the last seven months, and that's just Atlanta. It's been even worse farther west. Denver even got a dirty bomb..."

"What?"

"The explosion didn't do much damage, but there's been a few cases of radiation sickness. The worst is the fear. Everyone's so afraid all the time. Nobody knows where the terrorists will strike next."

She shook her head again.

"Enough of doom and gloom. Ethan, you're back!"

He noticed the unspoken question; How long? Is it for good this time?

"I have a month, unless I'm recalled early," he said. Elsie nodded thoughtfully.

"Well then... I'll let you get some sleep, but you must eat first." He was about to protest, but she cut him off.

"There's no use Ethan. You're scrawny!" She put on a stern face that held for a few seconds before breaking into a fond smile. "You're going to eat, and that's that."

49.

Ethan sat alone on the couch, while an old movie played on the TV. His mind though, was elsewhere. He kept thinking back on what had happened on Ceres, on Mars and of course, on Titan. His mind wandered back to Tsinga, the Lumin who had sworn fealty to him when surrendering. He wondered where she was now. Probably on the Lumins' home world, wherever that might be. Then he thought of the fighters who had attacked them on Titan, how political strife and a stirring of factions had turned deadly, until Ethan's squad of legionnaires had put an end to it, at least for the time being. He remembered Legionnaire Green's tears, upon hearing that his sisters had been killed and his father severely wounded by terrorists on Earth, while he was fighting aliens on Titan. He remembered Tom Lowry on Ceres, badly wounded and in pain, and he remembered seeing Eileen's name on the casualty list, his first in more than one way. Malika... He had actually thought they had something special, but that was gone. During those last months on Titan they had slowly began to act less awkward around each other, and he considered her a friend now. Thoughts of legionnaires, dead and alive, kept swirling through his head, and he realized he wasn't paying attention to the movie at all. He got up to get a beer from the fridge. Elsie wouldn't be back until sometime tomorrow; she was working night shifts this week.

The doorbell rang, and he started. He had only fixed it yesterday, and he reminded himself to set the volume down just a bit. Wouldn't want to wake the neighbors. He walked up to the door, not knowing what to expect. For a moment he considered taking out his sidearm. Tensions were high, and if the regular forces decided to take on the Legion for real... He decided against it, and opened the door ajar, without removing the security chain.

"Can I come in? It's freezing cold outside."

Helena Neuwijnkel flashed him a broad smile.

Her eyes glittered and her hair was loose, flowing across her shoulders. Her uniform was newly pressed and fit perfectly. Ethan removed the security chain and opened the door. He hardly noticed her recently acquired insignia, a big black O above the bold square of heavy infantry, as she stepped inside. She walked into the living room and Ethan followed her, eyes glued to her butt. She turned, and he quickly moved his eyes up to her face. She laughed softly and pursed her lips.

"We've never..." she began.

Ethan took a step toward her. Words were futile, but he repeated hers nevertheless.

"We've never..." he whispered hoarsely.

Helena opened the topmost button of her blouse.

"I think maybe we should..." she half-whispered.

She opened another button.

"You think we should?" Ethan took another step toward her.

She opened a third button and pulled the blouse above her head and tossed it on the floor.

"I want to..."

"I want to, too..."

They kissed and began tearing the clothes off each other. Helena playfully bit his ear and whispered throatily,

"I'll give you a night to remember."

~

End of Legion Rising, Legionnaire Series, Book 2

Dear Reader

Legion Rising is the second installment in the Legionnaire Series, and I hope you enjoyed reading it. I'd love it if you continue to tag along for more space adventures with Ethan, Ariel, Julian, and the rest of the legionnaires.

If we don't already know each other, you can find me on Facebook, Twitter, Goodreads and on my website and blog. To make sure you don't miss out on anything, I invite you to join my inner circle by signing up to my somewhat irregular newsletter. You can do so by going to **christensenwriting.com** and sign up there.

As soon as you join up, I'll send you a free e-book. As a member of my inner circle, you will always be the first to know about new releases, and sometimes I even have special treats that you will find nowhere else. And let me assure you, your email address is safe with me - I promise not to spam you, sell or give away your email address. Looking forward to having you on board!

A quick note on reviews

Before you leave this book, I would like to ask you a favor.

In the new world of publishing, word of mouth may be the most important factor in a story finding its readers. For an independent author, such as me, this is especially important. If you enjoyed this book, please consider leaving a review. It doesn't matter if it's short; the fact that someone read it, and liked it, could mean the difference between another reader deciding to try it, or moving on to the next one. And it would be much appreciated.

About the author

I am an independent author, living just outside of Oslo, Norway. I write mainly science fiction, although I occasionally try my hand at fantasy. In my writing I try to combine my interests in science and politics with psychology, in which I incidentally have a Master's degree. (never thought I'd use it in this way!) I think my diverse interests and background gives me a few valuable perspectives that enhance my writing, and although my main literary interest lies in the scifi and fantasy sphere, I enjoy a good thriller or horror now and then.

From my reviews I learn that different readers enjoy different aspects of my books. Some enjoy the adventure; some find a message of hope, while others have said they find themselves nodding as they read it. One of my favorite reviews for Exodus, my first published work, said that *"This book is science fiction in great form. It doesn't just make you think about the future, it really makes you think about the world around you today"*

When I was a kid, I used to draw cartoons and make up all kinds of stories. It still took many years before I learned one can actually reach an audience all over the world, and even longer before I finished a book. Now I just can't wait to get to the keyboard, my head filled with stories, just waiting to be told!

I love the process of writing, and sometimes it almost feels like I'm living the adventures of my characters. I guess that's the trick; to write the books you'd love to read (although I don't presume to know the formula for a bestseller - yet).

So what's my best book so far?

The next one...

~

See my complete bibliography on
christensenwriting.com/books

Connect with me online

Website: christensenwriting.com

Blog: christensenwriting.com/blog

Twitter: twitter.com/achr75

Facebook: facebook.com/christensenwriting